I0638070

On the
Western
Trail

A Western Quest Series Novel

On the Western Trail

A Western Quest Series Novel

Stephen L. Turner

SUNSTONE
PRESS

SANTA FE

© 2012 by Stephen L. Turner
All Rights Reserved.

No part of this book may be reproduced in any form or by any electronic or
mechanical means including information storage and retrieval systems
without permission in writing from the publisher, except by a reviewer
who may quote brief passages in a review.

Sunstone books may be purchased for educational, business, or sales promotional use.
For information please write: Special Markets Department, Sunstone Press,
P.O. Box 2321, Santa Fe, New Mexico 87504-2321.

Book and Cover design ›Vicki Ahl
Body typeface › Book Antiqua
Printed on acid-free paper
☯

————————————————————————————————

Library of Congress Cataloging-in-Publication Data

Turner, Stephen L., 1957-
   On the western trail : a western quest series novel / by Stephen L. Turner.
      p. cm. -- (Western quest ; 7)
   ISBN 978-0-86534-867-7 (softcover : alk. paper)
   1. Cattle trails--West (U.S.)--Fiction. I. Title.
   PS3620.U76596O67 2012
   813'.6--dc23
                              2012013038

————————————————————————————————

WWW.SUNSTONEPRESS.COM
SUNSTONE PRESS / POST OFFICE BOX 2321 / SANTA FE, NM 87504-2321 /USA
(505) 988-4418 / ORDERS ONLY (800) 243-5644 / FAX (505) 988-1025

Dedication

THIS BOOK, ALONG WITH the one before it and the one to follow, is dedicated to the memory of Aaron Lloyd Turner, my great-grandfather. He was a remarkable man. Returning from the War Between the States to find his family in financial straits, Aaron did what many young men of his day did. He grabbed a horse and a rope and started gathering unclaimed cattle to drive to the northern markets. Following the availability of maverick cattle, Aaron eventually ends up on Pecan Bayou, one of the tributaries of the Colorado River on the far western frontier. This story follows the great cattle culture of Texas as it reaches its zenith at Dodge City, Kansas, the terminal of the Western Trail. But the writing is already on the wall, as every strand of barbed wire is strung and every mile of railroad track laid foretells the end of this unique era in American history. Aaron adapted, became part of the changing culture, and survived to prosper in the shadow of the Plains.

Acknowledgements

THANKS ARE DUE TO MY cousin, Ella Turner Bullard, youngest daughter of Aaron Allinson (Al) Turner, and the granddaughter of Aaron Lloyd Turner, for her meticulous research and willingness to share family history. She is the last Turner living in Callahan County. The content of this book has been enriched by the editing and the careful proofreading of my parents, Aaron Lynn Turner, PhD, the grandson of Aaron Lloyd Turner, and Doris Alene Combs Turner. Thanks are due to my friend, Kim Hays, PhD, for sharing his expertise of the walking beam cable tool drilling rig. I studied a functioning model on display at the Panhandle Plains Museum at West Texas A&M University. This series of books, now in the seventh volume, would not have been possible without the unending support of my wife, Roberta Lyles Turner.

1

July 1875, Callahan County, Texas
Riding with the Rangers

THE BUGLE'S SHARP NOTES pierced the hot, humid morning air sounding "Recall." Almost immediately we heard a brisk exchange of gunfire, as rifle shots rang out to our west.

"Come on!" I yelled to my seven companions. We galloped to the sound of the guns.

A band of about thirty Comanche braves were waging a fighting retreat, fleeing north with their women and children. The half dozen travois carrying their goods slowed them down, but the men were making a strong rear guard fight to let them get away.

Captain William J. Maltby commanded Company E, Frontier Battalion of the Texas Rangers. We had been recruited to support the Rangers as had other ranchers in the area. The Frontier Battalion was making a clean sweep to remove the last pockets of Indians in Callahan County. We had travelled in a wide mounted line along Pecan Bayou, turning north at Lytle's Gap at the corner of our ranch.

The Comanche had situated themselves in a good defensive position; they would be mighty hard to knock loose. We could see dust rising to the north as the women, children and old ones rode away. The braves carried repeating rifles and knew how to use them. There weren't enough Rangers and volunteers to force them out. Pecos reined in near the Captain and dismounted.

"Beggin' the Captain's pardon, sir. Pecos Wade, volunteer. I speak good Comanche. If they agree to join their families and keep travelin' past the Red River, would you be willin' to let them go?"

"You musta been a good ol' Johnny Reb, too, son."

"Yessir. Texas Fifteenth Regiment, Company F."

"I don't trust them Injuns as far as I could throw an anvil."

"Sir, that's their families raisin' dust up north. If they break off the fight, keep their rifles and horses and let us escort them to the Nations, would you give it a try?"

"Well, at this point, we don't have a lot to lose. You goin' alone?"

"No sir! I want you and my friend, Aaron Turner, to go with me."

Pecos rode into sight with a white rag tied to his rifle. He held it horizontal above his head, a universal symbol of truce among the Plains Indians. The gunfire from the Comanche immediately stopped. A stout middle-aged brave swung onto his horse with a white rag tied to his Winchester, just like Pecos. When they got within shouting distance they parlayed a bit, then turned and rode apart.

"Captain, if you and Aaron would follow me, he said he'd talk."

The speaker's name was Broken Nose for obvious reasons. Two more braves accompanied him. Comanche was an incomprehensible language to me, but I could follow some of the hand talk.

"If they can keep their guns and horses, they'll take their families north of the Red River. We're to follow just out of rifle range. Broken Nose pledges his band won't return south of the river, even to raid for horses."

"You believe that ol' heathen?"

"No, sir. But I told him if he lies, we'll ride into the Nations until we find his camp and kill his family. He takes that real serious."

It seemed my family had enjoyed little peace since my father, Aaron Turner, first came to Texas in 1817. I was the youngest of a long line of children. I had been born Aaron Lloyd Turner in 1850, the year before my father died. My mother, Nancy, and my older siblings raised me to be pretty independent. I had enlisted in the Confederate Army at age twelve, along with my older brothers, David and Noah. David lay buried in Chicago, a victim of Camp Stephen Douglas. My brother, Noah, hadn't been seen or heard from since 1872. He had left for the buffalo hunting grounds along the Republican River. I had a sister, Mary Ann, who was married to Pickney Hawkins back in Limestone County, along with my mother, my half-brother, Marcus King and his wife, Glynna, and David's orphaned daughter, Alice. Pecos didn't have any family left after the war and had just become part of ours.

We had returned to a world turned upside down by Reconstruction. Catching maverick cattle and driving them north to trade for Yankee silver dollars had kept the wolf away from the door.

I had put together a good ranch on the North Fork of Pecan Bayou in Callahan County where we ran good crossbred cattle on homestead and free range land, making frequent trips back to Groesbeck to check on Mother. It was a hard life, but it had proven to be profitable. Even though we had to deal with outlaws, Indians and the dangers of the frontier, it was a life I loved.

We trailed the Comanche north about thirty miles a day. The second night, we made camp at the ruins of Fort Phantom Hill. Inconsistent water sources had caused the fort to be abandoned, but the tidy stone buildings provided good shelter. Pecos, who was part Comanche, said spirits roamed the fort at night. Captain Maltby rotated two Rangers at a time in shifts all night to keep an eye on the Indians.

A messenger rode ahead to alert Fort Griffin of what was happening. Broken Nose's band made camp on the banks of the Clear Fork of the Brazos. We positioned ourselves between them and the unruly buffalo hide hunters who lived near the fort.

We skirted wide of Seymour and Vernon. Mr. C. F. Doan at Doan's Store and Crossing met with Broken Nose. He told him he had men who watched the river for many miles. If he heard Broken Nose returned, he would send for the Rangers. Mr. Doan told us that Quannah Parker had brought his band of four hundred Quahadi Comanche to Fort Sill in June. That had been the last major war band outside of the reservation. Parker was perhaps the greatest of the Comanche chiefs, but he was a man of his word.

_____

John Lytle was the man who had earlier found a pass through the Callahan Divide. He had blazed a trail following good water sources across north Texas and western Oklahoma all the way to Dodge City, Kansas. In August 1875, he succeeded in driving a herd of three thousand five hundred head of cattle up the newly named Western Trail. There had been sharp skirmishes with Comanche, Cheyenne and Arapaho along the trail. Dodge had welcomed him royally. The opening of the new trail and the security of the now vacant plains would propel the cattle business in Texas to incredible new heights.

2

March, 1876, Limestone County, Texas
Reunion of the Unreconstructed

WINTER WAS ON ITS DEATH bed as spring was resurrecting itself once again in Limestone County. The cold rains had awakened the dormant native grasses and wild flowers. The delicate reborn life shouldered its way through the rocky soil. Momma was starting the spring cleaning, beating rugs and scrubbing floors and walls.

My niece, Alice, was thirteen, plain as a mud fence, and prone to whine and complain. I loved her because she was David's daughter, but it was hard to like her. Pecos claimed Alice was so ugly she had given his best horse the colic and could curdle fresh milk on a cold day. Mother had promised to raise her, and did her best.

Captain Tyus, my company commander during the War of Northern Aggression, was one of the five survivors of the one hundred and twenty men of the Texas Fifteenth Regiment, Company F to return home. He was also one of the finest men I knew. He and his wife rolled up in a fine black buggy drawn by matching black mares late one Friday afternoon.

"Captain, what are you and Mrs. Tyus doing here in Groesbeck?"

"I came to sign the deed on some land here and over in Leon County. I've already sold my place near Waco."

I was shocked. "Sir, what are you plannin' to do?"

"I bought an office building with living quarters in the second story. I plan to practice law part-time. I'm hoping to buy some choice cattle country in Callahan County." I just stood there with my mouth hanging open.

"Son, are you going to invite us in or leave us out here on the porch?"

"Sorry, Cap! Ya'll come on in the house!"

Captain Tyus gave me a big hug and Mrs. Tyus gave me a lady-like little kiss on the cheek. "We're going to be neighbors, Aaron. We're starting a new community to be called Belle Plain about six miles north of you across the Callahan Divide. The Dawsons, the Carters, the Shepards, and the Webbs are moving, too. Zachary Barton convinced his parents he was old enough to strike out on his own, but he'll be living with the Webbs. We want to establish a college there. I plan to teach English and the Law. Mr. Dawson has agreed to teach basic agriculture and animal husbandry. Mrs. Dawson and Mr. Carter will teach the sciences and math. Lisa Webb hopes to teach literature and Mrs. Shepard will offer home economics. Matt Dawson is going to set up a blacksmith shop. All of the families plan to raise cattle. What do you think?"

I sat grinning and speechless. My favorite people in the world would all be there in one place. "Mother, what about you and Alice?"

"We're quite happy here near Marcus, son."

"When will all this happen, Captain?"

"Aaron, we plan to leave as soon as we get the claims filed and the wagons loaded. You'll have neighbors by summer."

———

Captain Tyus filed on two sections of choice homestead land and bought eight more. It had live water, beautiful native grass and enough timber to be pretty. The Carters got four sections, one for both parents, and one each for Luke and Levi, who were now over twenty-one. The Dawsons filed for three sections and bought seven more. Jake was only nineteen and two years too young to file a claim. The Shepards got two sections of cow country and a quarter section of land that looked like it had farming potential.

Kelly Webb got a section for himself and one for his wife, Lisa. Somehow, he managed to get one for each of his three daughters and another for Little Jake. They were all short of twenty-one years old.

"Kelly, I know not a one of those kids is twenty-one. How'd you get those extra homestead sections?" I asked.

He reached deep into the side pocket of his bib overalls and pulled out a piece of blue carpenter's chalk. "Little Jake, come here, boy." Kelly picked up the bottom of Jake's shoe and carefully wrote the numeral twenty-one. "I had to swear each of 'em was over twenty-one!" I had to laugh at his devilish resourcefulness.

———

On April 15, 1875, I led twenty-four wagons and a large herd of mixed livestock from McLennan County headed west for a new home in Callahan County. The wagons held crates of squealing hogs and squawking chickens, fruit tree saplings wrapped in damp burlap, groceries, clothes, furniture and farm equipment. On the bottom of the loads were lumber and sheet metal. Milk cows plodded along, tied to the back of the wagons. The canvas was up on the wagon bows to protect their precious cargoes. There was room for riders only on the hard wagon seats, leaving many to follow along on horseback.

The Brazos was up, so we paid the ferryman to take the heavily loaded wagons across the swirling green water. It took a dozen trips to get them all safely on the west bank. The livestock herd managed to swim across without any problems.

The wagon train looked something like a travelling circus. Children laughed and ran beside the lumbering wagons, while a lively variety of barking dogs chased along with them. Every day held something new around each bend of the long dusty road. Supper was one great potluck dinner where a person could sample the fare and graze their way along the dinner line. The children played in the cool of the evening, the men spun tall tales, and the women gossiped just a bit. Matt and Jake played their guitar and fiddle nearly every night.

Once across the Colorado, the sense of excitement increased each day. We followed Pecan Bayou northwest into unsettled wilderness. Signs of civilized life slowly disappeared as the beautiful cattle country opened up before us. It had been two days since we had seen a cabin. The final night's camp was on my ranch at the foot of the Callahan Divide.

The grade at Lytle's Gap was pretty steep for such heavily loaded wagons. The mules were double-teamed for the trip up, with the process repeated until all the wagons reached the top. The grade on the northern slope was not so steep. The brakes were able to keep the wagons from running away. Once across the Divide, it was only six miles to the site they had chosen for Belle Plain. Here, all the creeks and streams found their way more or less north to the Brazos River, while south of the Divide everything eventually flowed into the Colorado River. The land they had chosen was beautiful pasture land covered with a blanket of thick native grasses and flowers. There were pecan, hackberry, live oak and cottonwood trees in abundance.

On reaching Belle Plain, they each drove their wagons to their predetermined places, then walked or rode back to Captain Tyus' wagons. They held a prayer and song service there on the frontier. A new town was born.

———————

The settler's cattle quickly found themselves at home on the lush prairie. Once the newcomers got squared away, we decided to gather any wild cattle we could find in the area. With a full crew, we were able to sweep the country south of the Divide pretty carefully for mavericks. Matt stayed behind to get his blacksmith shop set up. We weren't going to be out long enough to need the chuck wagon, so Kelly and Little Jake stayed in Belle Plain and started to frame up a house with Zach to help him. Luke, Levi, Kyle, Jake, Pecos and I started where Pecan Bayou ran into the Colorado. We spread out to drive any mavericks to the northwest toward the ranch. We had one pack mule with some food and cooking gear. Jake kept us in bacon, cornbread and coffee.

We found quite a few longhorns of all types, colors and sizes. They stayed loosely bunched ahead of us. Within five days, we had a mixed herd of about two hundred head. Once they passed the large cedar post that marked my southeast corner they encountered our tame crossbreds and began to settle down.

We drove the cattle in large groups to the working pens, which had been enlarged and rebuilt to be horse high, bull strong and hog tight. We sorted off the orejanos, those cattle with unnotched ears.

Pecos eased into the pen on a stout brown horse. He could throw a hoolihan even better than he could throw a rope overhead. The braided rawhide was deadly accurate at that range with the underhand throw. He looped the horns of a big tiger-stripe bull. Kyle was right behind him with a double hock catch that sent the bull to the ground with a thump and a bellow. Jake ran up on foot and quickly threw a few snug wraps around his front feet with a pigging string. With the bull secured, Levi ran in with a hot branding iron to burn the Rafter T on his left hip and the upside-down T road brand on his left ribs.

"Jake, you notch his ears. Soon as he's done, Luke, you and Levi castrate him."

The boys worked with practiced skill. I walked out and poured kerosene and sulphur down the bull's back to kill ticks. Jake released the angry brute's front feet and pulled a little slack in the rope, just as the boys did on his back feet.

"Run for it! This ol' boy's mad as a hornet."

The heavy bull struggled to free himself of the loosened rope and staggered to his feet. He was none too happy about his rude treatment and lost breeding ability. He swayed unsteadily until he focused his eyes on Pecos and his horse. Pecos spurred his horse through the suddenly opened gate and the bull charged after him. The big bruiser stopped, pawed dirt, and slung snot everywhere, before giving up and trotting off toward the cattle grouped along the creek.

"Another satisfied customer!" Pecos laughed.

The process was repeated hour after hour from too early to too late each day until all the mavericks had been worked. The Pecan Bayou country had been swept clean. We had cut back a few cows with brands and sent the boys to drive them back to where we found them. We didn't know who they belonged to, but they were surely strays. An honest man didn't keep cattle with another man's brand on them.

———————

Matt had supervised the building of some similar pens near Belle Plain that the families there would share for working their stock. We helped work the country north of the Divide until a hundred and seventy head had been gathered. We left those for Matt and the Belle Plain boys to handle, as Pecos and I had our own work to do.

I rode over to compare notes with Captain Tyus. "What's the tally, Aaron?"

"Cap, I got five hundred and three head ready to send to market. We got four hundred and thirteen from you. The Dawsons have got two hundred and fifteen, the Shepards one hundred and eight, the Carters sixty-seven, and Kelly is throwin' in twenty-three. That's one thousand two hundred and twenty-nine head of home raised cattle, mostly steers and a few barren cows. We caught three hundred and seventy-three mavericks. Seventy-three are too young to send and a hundred and twelve are breeding age cows. That leaves one hundred and ninety-eight stags and old cows to add to the trail herd. Let me add it all up. That's one thousand four hundred and twenty-seven head ready for Dodge City."

As agreed, on June first, all the various cattle were thrown together at Belle Plain for our departure up the long trail on June third, 1876. It was the first herd to leave from Belle Plain, but it would not be the last.

3

June 3, 1876, Belle Plain, Callahan County, Texas
Buffalo hides and buffalo soldiers at Fort Griffin

KYLE SHEPARD HAD BEEN with me as a scrawny teenager on the first drive in 1866 and every year since then. He was a grown man now with a grown man's problem.

"Hold on, Kyle!" Pull his head around! Use the inside spur!" The sorrel gelding was bucking with a sunfish motion. Kyle had one hand on the horn and his other pulling the reins hard to the left trying to turn him into a tight left-hand circle. The red horse was sky busting like a champion. He finally came down with a snort and took off at a gallop. Kyle whipped him across the rump to keep him running. Every time the horse tried to slow down he would spur him back into a gallop. He let the horse ease into a lope, then a trot, and finally, a very tired walk. Dirty lather covered the sorrel's neck, sides and rear. Kyle, much worse for the wear, had won the war with the rank cow horse.

The other hands hooted and clapped for Kyle while Jake ran up and caught the horse by the bridle. When Kyle stepped down he was a little wobbly. That young horse had given him all he wanted and then some.

We didn't have any more trouble that morning as we headed the spare horses and market cattle over Lytle's Gap to Belle Plain. The other cattle had been gathered and were ready to go. Kelly had my chuck wagon freshly painted and fully stocked. Little Jake was going as cook's helper and wrangler.

"Captain Tyus, looks like the Belle Plain bunch is ready to go."

"Morning, Aaron. Ready and eager. All of the horses and mules have new shoes, and the chuck wagon is loaded. Even Kelly's in a good mood."

"That'll be the day! Somebody give him a year's supply of tobacco? Pecos got all our stock shod. Kyle had to take that sorrel horse he's ridin' to school this mornin'. Other than that, we're ready to roll. I guess we'll see you when we get back to Texas in a few months."

"Biscuit, get that wagon rollin'! Little Jake, head the remuda in behind your Daddy. Pecos, move 'em out!" The dust rose in wisps from the thick prairie on the trail to Clyde. We pushed the cattle until nearly dark and bedded them south of town. Tired cows were less likely to run.

We made the trip to Fort Griffin in easy stages, grazing the cattle along the way. Pecos was at the left point, as was his position of honor as segundo. Matt had earned his place at right point. Zach, Luke, Levi, Jake and Kyle rotated around from flank to drag. Little Jake did just fine with the remuda.

When we got to Fort Griffin, we bedded the cattle down east of the fort and town in some good pasture among the cottonwood trees on the south side of the Clear Fork of the Brazos. "Pecos, keep a lid on things here while I go see the army post commander to ask about the Indian situation. Keep everybody out of town until I get back. That includes you, compadre."

———————

"I'm here to see the post commander, soldier."

"Well, ya might say we're a wee bit busy now, lad. What are ya wantin' anyway, ya damn Johnny Reb?"

"A little courtesy for starters, Sergeant."

"You're in the wrong place for that. Tell me your business so I can get ya outta here before the Colonel comes back."

Feeling my face flush red, I asked, "How are Indian conditions between here and Fort Supply?"

"Are ya deaf and dumb, or just plain stupid? A buffalo outfit got shot up comin' back from the Canadian River. Killed the two men who owned it, but the skinners got back with the mules, wagons and hides. They tore up those Cheyenne and Arapaho pretty good with those big .50 caliber Sharps."

"Yeah, I know. I may buy their outfit. What are the Arapaho and Cheyenne doin' this far south?"

"Did ya get hit in the head or was ya born stupid? There's a new reservation between the North Fork of the Red and the Washita River. Anythin' else ya gotta know?"

"What's your name, Sergeant?"

"First Sergeant Clancy O'Malley, ya yellow-bellied traitor. What's it to ya?"

I held my temper and stomped out the door and rode back to the herd.

"There it is. Cooper and Nixon Trading Post, Tavern and Inn. Look at those big fine Studebaker freight wagons. That's the best they make. They've got the buffalo hides piled up and tied down."

"The mules are around back. Come have a look. They got twenty of the best draft mules this side of the Mississippi."

"The harness is almost new, too. This is a nice set up."

A tall thin red-headed woman stepped out of the back door of the trading post with a double barreled shotgun. She wore a long dress with a wide leather belt and a holstered Colt. "Them's my mules and gear. State your bidness."

I looked at the shotgun and knew she was serious. "Are you Mrs. Nixon?"

"Yah. What's that to you?" The shotgun was leveled at my chest.

"Ma'am, we heard about your husband and brother in law gittin' kilt by the Cheyenne. We're right sorry. We come to see if you would wanna sell the freight outfit."

"Tamara, git the kids and come on out here."

Her sister was shorter and darker, but looked just as tough. She wore a pistol over her long shirt and carried a shotgun. Four teenagers crowded around, pushing to the front. Like their mothers, they were also armed to the teeth.

"This is my sister, Tamara Cooper, her boy, Tate, and her girl, Tory. These two red-heads are mine, Kirby and Keenan."

"Ma'am." I tipped my hat as Matt did. "I was wonderin' if you would be wantin' to sell your freight outfit, wagons, mules, harness and all. We're takin' a herd to Dodge City. I could sell the hides and back haul freight and trade goods."

"What are ya offerin', Tex?"

"Sorry for not introducin' myself. I'm Aaron Turner from Callahan County. This is Matt Dawson."

"Well, I guess ya oughta be right proud of yourself, but I don't give a darn who ya are or where you're from. I asked ya what you're offerin'."

Matt gave me a sideways glance. He knew I had tied onto a genuine brush bustin' mamma longhorn, and she was on the prod. "Could we walk out among the mules to look 'em over a little closer?"

"Suit yourself, Tex. I got work to do. When ya got somethin' to talk to me about come around front. I got a winder that looks out back, so don't you try pullin' no stunts with me, Rooster."

"You roped ya a real cimarrone, Aaron. Glad I could be so much help."

"Ah, shut your pie hole and open that corral gate."

We looked for sore shoulders, swollen hocks, worn teeth, bad feet and blind eyes. This was as good a set of genuine draft mules as I had seen in a long time. "Come on, let's go see if the wagons are as good as the mules."

There were five nearly new Studebaker wagons, the heaviest they sold. All of them were as solid as rock, and the paint wasn't even faded. The wheels had solid, tight spokes and tight iron rims. It was obvious they had been kept greased. Under the wagons were spare tongues, axles and wheels. Each wagon had a tool box mounted on the side with everything needed to service or repair them. Another side-mounted box held brand new wagon tarps that didn't look like they had ever been put on the bows. Four of the wagons were mounded as high as the hides could be stacked and tied tightly down. The last wagon had only a small load of hides. The Cheyenne must have attacked before they finished their load.

Finally, we checked the harnesses and tack. It must have been bought new with the wagons. Everything in near perfect condition. The only sign that they had been used at all was some sweat stains on the leather. "Let's go talk to Kelly and Pecos and see what they think we oughta offer."

"Well, I guess I know as much about mules as anybody on the drive. I ain't seen any better since I left Arkansas. As far as the wagons go, everybody knows Studebaker is the best there is. All the harness and tack looks good." Kelly turned to Pecos. "Whatta you think?"

"I sure ain't gonna argue with you about mules, wagons, or harness. I'm a top cowhand. We leave that foolery to the cooks and such."

"Well, thanks for all your help, Pecos! I'm gonna offer a hundred dollars each for the mules and hundred and a quarter for the wagons, with another two fifty for all the harness and tack."

Pecos grinned. "Boss, that sounds about right. I jes see one problem. You ain't got that much money."

"I'm gonna give her a draft off my bank in Waco. I can cover it, but if she wants, I'll trade out the note for hard money when we git back from Dodge."

I pitched the idea to them, and they seemed to kick it back and forth. Robin Nixon spoke up. "The price is as good, or better, than we can git anywhere around here. I don't like the idea of the bank draft. Can you prove you're good for it?"

Kyle had been hanging back listening. He walked up and whispered to me.

"Yeah, that's a good idea. Ma'am, we'll telegraph the bank to prove the note is good. You hold it until I get back and I'll swap it back for Yankee silver dollars."

"Keenan, go find them good-for-nothin' Beasley boys. Kirby, you cut along with Mr. Turner to the telegraph office."

Soon, Kirby and I returned with a telegram confirming that the draft was in fact good for the amount mentioned, and much more if necessary. About that time, two unwashed boys in worn out clothes came running up with Keenan.

"Aaron, we almost got us a deal except two things. First, I want you to haul those hides to Dodge City and sell 'em for the best price you can git. You haul 'em free since I'm holding your paper. Second, you take our three boys along as teamsters. They know how to handle a team. The goin' rate is a dollar a day plus grub. You still got two wagons without drivers. This is Tyler and Tanner Beasley. The Comanche killed their parents and they ain't got no family or place to go. You take 'em on, too, and you got a deal."

Robin could drive a hard bargain. I knew I had met my match and agreed. Kelly started checking the boys out on the wagons as the two sisters fitted the Beasley boys out with clothes and bedrolls for the trip. They also gave me my first grocery order for my new freight business.

_____

In spite of my best efforts, Matt and Pecos had gone to visit "Fort Griffin-Under-The-Hill" before we left. It was known to be one of the roughest, most dangerous, filthy little pot-hole buffalo hunting towns in the west. To make things worse on our account, there weren't only buffalo hunters, skinners, gamblers, thieves, soiled doves and killers, but the fort itself was garrisoned by Negro soldiers. We had not had good experiences with these "Buffalo Soldiers" during Reconstruction. It was still a real sore subject with a lot of Texans. About midnight I could hear a ruckus coming from the direction of the center of town. I didn't like the sound of it and grabbed my clothes. As I passed the Nixon's combination store, tavern and inn, Robin stepped out on the front porch. "Them 'Buffalo Soldiers' has got two of your drovers hemmed up, givin' 'em a bad beatin'. You're gonna need help!"

I ran back to camp. "All hands and the cook!" My drovers started jumping out of their bedrolls in every direction. "Matt and Pecos are in trouble. Get dressed fast. No guns!"

Kelly, Little Jake, Zach, Kyle, Luke and Levi were running behind me. When we reached the Nixon Store, Robin was passing out axe handles. "You can borry 'em for nothin', but if ya bust 'em, they're fifty cents apiece."

As we were getting our hickory handles, Kirby, Kennan, Tyler and Tanner came rushing out onto the porch, too. "Grab one and come on, boys!"

The noise was coming from in front of "The Bull's Head Saloon." A lantern hanging from the branches of a dead tree across the road cast a ring of pale yellow light. Inside the circle stood a large group of black soldiers surrounding Pecos and Matt, who stood back to back. The soldiers were under the direction of the insolent Irish sergeant. They were taking turns throwing punches. Pecos and Matt were able to deflect some of them, but many were hitting home.

From the shadows beyond the weak light, I did my best to sound like an angry Yankee officer. "Officer on parade! Ten hut!"

The startled soldiers stood at attention. "Sergeant O'Malley, what is the meaning of this?"

"Why, sir, we're just havin' a friendly little scuffle with these Johnny Rebs."

"Is this a military or a private affair, Sergeant?"

"Oh, it's strictly private, sir. We can't see you back there in the dark, sir. Which officer are you?"

"Lieutenant, when we return to the fort, place Sergeant O'Malley under arrest for insubordination. Corporal, send for the Provost Guard on the double."

Kelly boomed out "Yes sir, Captain!"

"If this is a private matter, you soldiers will strip your blouses. I will not tolerate troopers of the United States Fourth Cavalry brawling in the street like buffalo skinners." Some of the soldiers started taking off their blue tunics, but quite a few could be seen trotting up the hill back to their quarters. "As you were, Sergeant O'Malley."

"Thank you, Captain."

The circle around Pecos and Matt was much smaller now. We spread in a circle in the darkness beyond the reach of the light from the smoking lantern until I was just behind O'Malley. "Now, give it to 'em, boys!"

We raised the Rebel yell and charged into the soldiers with a vengeance. The element of surprise and the axe handles made an effective combination. Pecos and Matt used the diversion to launch an attack of their own against their tormentors. Our revenge was quick and complete.

Keenan and Kirby brought clothes line from the store. We tied the battered and bleeding soldiers hand and foot. The Beasley boys fetched the nearly empty fifth wagon while the rest of the men tossed our captives like sacks of potatoes onto the thin pile of buffalo robes. We pulled their boots and brogans off and stuffed their dirty socks in their mouths to keep them quiet. Jake and Matt drove the wagon down to the bridge over the Clear Fork of the Brazos with their horses tied to the tailgate. They were to go about five miles and pull off the road with the wagon in the brush.

Kelly and Little Jake fixed a hurried breakfast of coffee, bacon and cornbread in the pre-dawn darkness. By the time we had eaten, it was light enough to see. We headed the wagons across the bridge, but Little Jake took the remuda directly across the river. The cattle dutifully followed the horses. Kirby had remembered to collect the axe handles and returned them to his mother.

We spotted Pecos and Matt's wagon about eight o'clock. I tied my horse to the tailgate and climbed into the crowded wagon bed. I plucked the sock from the sergeant's mouth. "Do you remember who you called a stupid yellow-bellied traitor, Sergeant?"

"So it was you?!"

"You and your colored soldiers was havin' a little rough fun with two of my men. We don't appreciate that much. Now I'm gonna make you an offer. If you and your men don't give us any more trouble, we'll take those socks out of your nasty mouths. My cook will fix a big pot of hot coffee, a pan of cornbread and fry up plenty of bacon. We'll give you your boots and let ya walk back to Fort Griffin."

"Or what, Johnny Reb?"

"We'll take you with us up the trail to Fort Supply, and tell 'em we caught some Yankee deserters."

"If you do that, they're liable to hang all of us."

"Yeah, I reckon you're right about that. I was kinda hopin' you'd take my first offer."

"Well, who could turn down a deal like that? Start the coffee."

"Now you won't tell the Provost about us. You tell him some of your troopers had a little too much to drink and you had to go gather 'em up."

"Aye. It's a deal. We never saw ya!"

"One last thing, Sergeant O'Malley. When we come back down the trail from Kansas, I'll buy the first round of drinks for you and your men."

"Alright, the first round is on you. You know, you make a pretty convincin' Yankee officer."

4

On the trail at last

WE HAD COMPLETELY BY-passed Throckmorton, then crossed the Prairie Dog Fork of the Brazos River near Seymour. We never even turned our eyes toward them. Towns had been nothing but trouble so far.

The Pease River was cool, crystal clear and only ankle deep near Vernon. Before I could stop him, Keenan had jumped off his wagon and headed upstream to get a drink.

"Boy, how'd that water taste?"

"Kinda like skunk piss, Boss, but I was thirsty. Somethin' wrong with it?"

"Any time you smell that, it means its alkali or gyp water. Don't drink it."

"Why not?"

"You'll be able to answer that yourself later." Those of us who had experience with gyp water grinned at Keenan's pending problem.

Kelly hollered down from his wagon. "That boy's gonna be mighty sorry, but maybe it'll improve his personality."

"Biscuit, how's Little Jake holdin' up?"

"He's sore from ridin' all day and tired from workin' so hard and sleepin' so little. It'll make him tough if it don't kill him. He was kinda impressed with all the doin's at Fort Griffin."

"Not every ten year old gits to be in an old-fashion brawl. Them colored soldiers sure got the worst of it."

Kelly spit tobacco at a lizard on the road and grinned at me. "His momma don't ever need to know nothin' about it neither."

Soon we saw Keenan's wagon trotting along without him in it. He was runnin' for the bushes as fast as he could go. When he came walking back, he had his shirt tied around his waist without any pants to be seen. "Whatever y'all do, don't never drink none of that gyp water. When it hits, it's done too late."

———

Doan's Store sat in a grove of mature cottonwood trees along with a few other buildings. It was the last piece of Texas we would see before crossing the Red River into the Nations. C. F. Doan had started a small business that was rapidly turning into a big one, and he was a fountain of information. He said cattle prices were good and buffalo hides were bringing top dollar for good flint hides like these. He wrote out a list of supplies he could use for the store and gave me two small sacks of mail, one destined for Fort Supply and the other for Dodge.

We bought Keenan some extra pants and summer drawers, although there weren't a lot of things that would fit a wormy twelve year old. He entertained Mr. Doan and some of his customers with an all too vivid account of the effects of drinking gyp water. Kelly picked up a few things for the drive and an armload of plug tobacco. He gummed it like a rat eats corn.

The more mature among the bunch took advantage of the last opportunity to partake of ardent spirits for a few hundred miles. The youngsters had beer or sasparilla.

"Aaron, before you leave, you need to know the Cheyenne and Arapahoe are in a pretty foul mood. You be extra careful once you cross the North Fork of the Red River all the way to the Washita. They mean business and I know they carry Winchesters. They bought 'em here."

———

The river was up and rolling muddy red water. I rode the crossing, but my horse had to swim most of the way. The cowboys stripped down to just their summer drawers and put their boots and clothes in the chuck wagon.

"Hup, mules!" Kelly cracked the whip over the backs of our four best bay mules. The current moved the wagon a short way down stream, but the mules were able to swim across and pull the wagon up the north bank. I didn't know much about how any of the four other boys would handle the big Studebaker wagons, but I should have. Zach had driven the wagon plenty when he had been Kelly's helper on the Chisholm Trail. He wouldn't have any trouble. The hides were bulky, but not overly heavy.

Tanner, the younger Beasley boy, was only twelve or thirteen. His wagon was the one that held just a partial load of hides. As his team hit the rushing red water he panicked and began to rein his mules to the left or upstream side. This immediately started the wagon turning parallel to the bank and straight against the current and it drifted downstream, even with the four mules swimming as hard as they could.

Pecos galloped to the edge of the river and swam his horse to the floundering wagon. Turning his horse loose to swim, he climbed onto the wagon box and took the reins from Tanner. He hauled hard on the right mules and whipped the left ones. The wagon began to swing at an angle across the current. A little more tugging, whipping and cussing and the team was headed for the north bank. They finally struggled out a quarter mile down river from where they had entered. Pecos had saved Tanner, the wagon and the mules.

I galloped up leading Pecos' horse. "Thanks, amigo. That was nearly a bad deal."

"Tanner, we ain't had time to make a freighter out of you yet, but we'll work on it. Don't blame yourself. It was my fault. Now gather up your reins and drive back to your spot in line."

Little Jake didn't have any trouble getting the horses across and the cows followed easily. They got soaked to the bone but swam like beavers.

———

"Kelly, what do ya think of our crew so far this year?"

He set down his coffee cup and directed a stream of brown juice at a horned toad. "You know I think the world of Pecos. He's as good a cowhand as ever roped a maverick. Matt's almost as good and sure can play that guitar. Jake's nearly growed and is nearly as good as Matt. Now that boy can make a fiddle sing like an angel. He's kinda my favorite since he used to be my helper way back in the day."

"Kyle has grown into a dependable man to have around who can get the job done. Luke and Levi were just drowned rats the first time we went up the trail in '66, but they growed up to be good hands. Zach Barton's makin' a good 'un, too. I hope he don't mind being stuck drivin' a wagon. Course I love havin' my own boy with me. Little Jake is gonna be a good man one day, too."

"What about the new boys? I don't hardly know 'em."

"Me neither. Them Beasley boys just seem glad to have some grub and a place out of the rain. Tate, Keenan and Kirby got the makin's for good teamsters. I guess they growed up around it."

Kelly wasn't just the cook. He was my friend. As far as I could figure, he was just shy of fifty, six foot seven, three hundred sturdy pounds, baldheaded and toothless. He had the ability to offer advice when I asked for it and the patience to bide his peace when I didn't ask.

Pecos was my strong right arm. He was twenty-seven, five foot nine and the best cowhand I knew. He was loyal to a fault and my closest friend.

I had ridden with Matt, Jake, Kyle, Luke and Levi for ten years. I had seen them grow from boys to good men. Zach hadn't been with us long, but he fit right in with the rest. They were like little brothers and I would take a bullet for any of them. I think they felt the same way. We were a tight outfit.

5

July 18, 1876, Big Elk Creek, Cheyenne and Arapaho Reservation, Indian Territory
Comanche Springs

WE CROSSED THE NORTH Fork of the Red River without incident. We were now in the recently established reservation of the Southern Cheyenne and their kinsmen, the Arapaho. Word was, they weren't too happy to be there. The east was bounded by red sandstone bluffs. A clear wide creek flowed at the foot of the bluffs. The creek bank was intermittently scattered with groves of pecan, cottonwood, elm, hackberry and oaks. Spreading out in green glory was a prairie five miles north to south and two miles wide, over six thousand acres of little bluestem, side oats grama, blue grama, curly mesquite, and buffalo grass. Islands of trees dotted the prairie. Mule deer and antelope grazed undisturbed in the distance. The cattle filled themselves on the rich pasture. I knew there was danger on this beautiful sea of grass.

"Pecos, I think we need to fort up."

"I'm with you, Boss. I'd put four wagons across the west, and one on the north and south. Picket the horses along the creek on a double picket line with hobbles. Pull all the boys inside. The herd isn't gonna go anywhere."

We wheeled and man-handled the wagons into place. We stacked crates and barrels along the wagon tongues, as well as excess buffalo hides, harness and tack.

Keenan, Kirby and Tate came wandering up. Kirby was about fourteen, skinny as a rail with dark red hair, freckles, and sober as a judge. "Aaron, the Indians who killed our fathers were Cheyenne and Arapaho. We reckon they came from here. We think there's a good chance it's the same bunch."

"Probably right."

"You may think we're just a bunch of little kids, but all three of us learned to shoot straight from huntin' buffalo. We ain't scared. You turn us loose and let us fight."

I smiled to myself. "Boys, these Indians are the real deal. You may get to do all the fightin' you want to do. You'll do exactly what I tell you to do, or I'll take your guns away. Do you understand?"

Most of us took advantage of the warm evening and the clean water for a swim and a much needed bath. Wet clothes were hanging haphazardly from the wagons when Kyle came galloping up.

"Aaron, we got company. Five Injuns are across from the herd signalin' somethin'."

"Everybody get dressed and grab your guns. Kyle, make sure everyone is in off the herd. Pecos, you're comin' with me."

The five Indians were mounted on good horses. They wore finely detailed beaded buckskins. All of them were tall handsome men with long hair flowing loose, with bows across their backs and Winchesters across their laps.

"Cheyenne?"

"Yeah, I think so. Aaron, look at that war lance. There's two fresh scalps. One is red, just the same color as the Nixon boys, the other is dark and curly like Tate's hair."

"Wohaw!" The owner of the war lance crowded his horse to the front and flashed five fingers twice.

Pecos signed that they were welcome to three head.

"Wohaw!" He showed ten fingers again.

"Tell him I said to go to hell!"

Quick as a flash, five Winchesters were trained on us. We raised our hands. The sound of rolling thunder crashed from behind us as three braves were knocked from their mounts by the Sharps Buffalo rifles. We used the confusion to gallop through the herd toward the protection of the rifles on the wagons. The remaining two Indians fired wild shots toward us and the wagons before wheeling away at a dead gallop.

As we approached the creek, I could see Tate, Kirby and Keenan lying across the tops of the wagons piled with hides holding their Sharps rifles. "Did you boys do that?"

"Dang sure did!" Keenan smiled.

"Good shootin'! You best be ready 'cause they'll be back."

———————

I quickly assessed our situation with Kelly, Pecos and Matt. The creek and the horses should provide a good defensive position. The front row of four wagons gave good cover. I left Tate and his cousins there with their Sharps and a Winchester each. The two wagons at the front corners were not too vulnerable as they would receive supporting cover from the other positions. On the flanks, I put Jake under the south wagon with Levi on top of the hides. Both had Winchesters and Colts. The north wagon had Tanner Beasley under it with a double barreled shotgun and a pistol with Luke on top of the wagon. I expected the first attack to come from the west, so I put Zach, Kyle and Tyler under those wagons.

We pulled the tarp off the chuck wagon and I arranged myself there on the northwest corner nestled in barrels and crates. The especially vulnerable places would be where the two rear wagon tongues met the picketed horses. We made a good barricade there and ran a head-high rope from the wagon bow to the trees the held the picket lines. It might knock anyone off their horse who tried to jump over the barricade. Matt and Pecos each took a corner. Kelly and Little Jake stood in the middle with double barreled shotguns to shoot any Indians that got through. The fire was out and full water buckets stood near each wagon.

"You boys on top of the wagons scoot back a little to get some protection from those stinkin' hides. Everybody make sure you got extra cartridges." I took a walk around to check everything. "Where the hell is Tate?"

Kirby pointed to the bluff behind us. "Tate's a good shot with a Sharps. He can hit 'em from a quarter of a mile."

Down from the red sandstone behind us Tate shouted "Here they come, thirty or more." An echoing boom indicated Tate had fired. I turned to see he was using crossed sticks to support the heavy rifle. I guess he did know how to shoot, but if the Cheyenne crossed the creek, he was going to be in a bad place.

With the shot came a nerve shattering war cry. The Cheyenne were lead by a chief in a beaded red shirt and a full war bonnet. They all wore paint. They raced on toward the wagons, weaving their way through the cattle. There was another boom from the bluff and a Cheyenne was knocked backwards from his horse. Keenan and Kirby were high enough they had a chance to shoot, but the moving targets and cattle made it tough. Both fired a few rounds. The Cheyenne recognized the threat, but pressed on at a trot to the wagons.

Tate's gun bellowed again and another attacker fell. Keenan fired again. With a bellow of pain, a big spotted steer fell dead. "Sorry, Boss!"

Realizing the cattle provided some protection, the Indians began to use their rifles in the general direction of the wagons. The shots scattered wildly, but a stray bullet pounded into a barrel next to me. Finally, the cattle parted and the war band came on full speed. The Nixon boys picked up their Winchesters; Kyle, Tyler and Zach were able to bring their guns to bear from under the wagons. Levi and Luke began to fire from the tops of the side wagons, although their fire attracted some shots from the attackers. They both were forced to retreat under the wagons.

The aggressors charged straight at the front wagons unleashing a withering fire. A lucky blast from Tyler's shotgun dropped a Cheyenne, and Kirby wounded another. The war band split and attacked both the north and south sides. Levi and Jake opened up a hot fire with their pistols from under the wagon. Matt stood ready with his Winchester at the corner, firing as fast as he could work the lever. Another Indian fell. On the north, Luke with a Colt and Tanner with a shotgun fired panicked shots that wounded two horses.

Pecos was ready at the corner with his Colt, but he was forced to take cover from the heavy rifle fire. A quick shot dropped a Cheyenne who had been knocked from his horse by the stretched rope. A boom and a puff of smoke from the bluff brought the end to the Indian threat on the north side.

The southern group swung out into the creek, but found the water too deep to maneuver. They joined the northern group as they all raced away to the safety of a grove of trees out of rifle range to the north. Five lay on the ground somewhere among the herd and five were scattered around the wagons. We were safe for the moment, but still outnumbered at least two to one. So far none of us had been hurt.

Realizing we were most vulnerable on the north and south sides, I shifted Kyle to support the north and Tyler the south. The Cheyenne charged headlong straight at the single wagon on the north. Pecos, Zach, Luke and Tanner fired everything they had, but only killed a horse. Two shots from Tate on the bluff missed their mark. As the angry warriors reached the wagons, they wheeled wildly. Two were able to slash the interfering rope and jumped the barrier defended by Pecos. Kelly and Little Jake's shotguns killed them both. The other warriors jumped from their horses and threw themselves under the north wagon. Before he could fire a shot, a Cheyenne slit Tanner's throat and swiftly turned on Luke. Luke's scream and pistol shot rang out at the same time splattering the attacker's brains and blood all over him.

Three Indians came at Pecos with their war clubs. He dropped two with his .44. A deafening boom and a rush of spent powder assaulted his face as Kelly's shotgun killed the third only two feet away.

My wagon on the corner proved to be a hot spot. I shot two Cheyenne as they jumped into the wagon, but a third had his club raised to crush my skull when a shot from Keenan knocked him completely out of the wagon. "We're even on the steer now, Boss!"

Red Shirt grabbed a horse and his surviving warriors followed him north at a gallop along the creek. A shot from Tate killed another. I was too stunned to fire. Tanner was dead, Luke was puking, and Pecos was calmly reloading. The war band split into two groups. The larger disappeared to the northwest. The smaller group headed upstream.

The Cheyenne appeared from the woods and tried to stampede

the cattle. They were busy grazing and simply scampered out of their way and refused to run away. Frustrated, the attackers began to shoot some of the cattle until the rumble of the Sharps drove them away. Kirby turned to yell congratulations to Tate when he screamed in horror. "Tate, behind you!"

Four dismounted Cheyenne swarmed over Tate. A round house blow from a stone war club connected solidly with the brave boy's head. His body, still clutching the Sharps, fell backwards off the bluff into the creek below. The Cheyenne were gone before we could react.

———

The horses and mules snorted and stomped nervously. Tyler, Kirby and Keenan were crying. Luke was retching under the wagon where Tanner and the Cheyenne lay dead.

"Sound off! Kelly, Little Jake?"

"We're okay, Aaron."

"Matt?"

"Yup."

The process continued. We had lost two. Kyle had been grazed by a bullet in his upper arm. We had survived, barely. "Kelly, I think we could all use some coffee."

"Pecos, would you fetch Tate's body from the creek?"

I pulled Tanner's bloody body out from under the wagon. We wrapped them both in their bedroll blankets. As the coffee got ready, Kelly produced a bottle of whiskey to sweeten the coffee of any who wanted it. I took a double dose while I patched up Kyle.

Without being asked, Jake and Matt dug two graves back from the creek. With help from Zach and Kyle, they carried the wrapped bodies and laid them in the freshly dug earth. They pulled out their fiddle and guitar and softly began playing "Shall We Gather at the River." We all drifted to the graves.

Tyler was taking the loss of his brother extremely hard. He didn't have another single living relative. Keenan and Kirby sobbed at the loss of their cousin, Tate. He had fought so bravely. It was my place to say something, but the words wouldn't come. With tear-stained pleading eyes, I looked to Kelly.

Spitting out his tobacco, he cleared his throat. "Y'all take off your hats. Let's pray."

Kelly led a thoughtful prayer and we sang "Amazing Grace" with the boys on the fiddle and guitar. I couldn't croak out a note. Straight, unpeeled cottonwood branches were carved with the appropriate initials and driven in the ground at the head of the graves. Red sandstone rocks were piled on top to keep the scavengers out. In ten years of trail driving these were our first losses. We gathered up the dead Cheyenne and laid them out side by side in the edge of the north woods. In the morning, the Indian dead were gone.

6

July 19, 1876, Comanche Springs, Big Elk Creek, Indian Nations
After the Whirlwind

TWO BOYS I HARDLY KNEW lay in freshly dug graves. I was in charge. Somehow, this had to be my fault. Without waiting for orders from me, Pecos regrouped the herd, got camp back in order and set guards for the night.

I could smell supper cooking but had no appetite. Pecos walked up and sat down next to me on the wagon tongue. "It wasn't your fault. You did everything anybody else would've done. Because of you, the rest of us are alive." I stared blankly back at Pecos. He was probably right, but I couldn't shake the feeling it had been my fault.

"Aaron, all of us, even me and Kelly, look up to you. This herd, these wagons, these men and boys are countin' on you to get 'em to Dodge. We likely wouldn't make it without you. We need you real bad right now, so shake it off and take charge so the others can see what you're made of. The hands need to see you got things firmly in control."

"Chows up! Come and get it before I throw it out!"

"Come on. Let's go see if we can choke down some of Ol' Biscuit's grub."

Levi came galloping in. "Aaron, there's soldiers comin'!"

As we stood up we could see a sergeant break off from his squad and lope toward the wagons.

"Hello the camp! Permission to ride in?"

I waved my hat. "Come on in, Sarge."

The white sergeant commanded a squad of ten colored privates and a corporal of the United States Second Cavalry. "Sergeant Hayden Alexander, sir. Who is in charge here?"

"I am. Aaron Turner, Callahan County, Texas. Signal your men to come on in. We got plenty of hot coffee, grub and grass for your horses."

"Beggin' your pardon, Mr. Turner. Do you want my troopers to eat inside your camp?"

"I don't understand, Sergeant. They got somethin' catchin'?"

"No, sir. They're Negros. Some folks object to eatin' with 'em."

"Well, I never noticed!" I smiled and turned to the sergeant. "I object to 'em bein' Yankees a whole lot more than I do them being colored. Hell, send 'em on in. We'll eat with anybody."

The soldiers drifted in, tied their horses and filled their plates. They sat near the picket line away from my men.

"Looks like you had trouble today. We patrol from Fort Supply to the North Fork of the Red River to keep an eye on the Cheyenne and Arapaho. Wish we had been here sooner."

"Me, too, Sergeant Alexander. We coulda used the help. They killed two of my crew and we killed nine or ten of them. They came close to killin' all of us."

"That's my job to escort herds through here. I ain't done you much good. I'd like for my platoon to stay with your outfit until you reach Fort Supply."

"We'll take all the help we can git, even from Yankees." I smiled to put him at ease. "Roll your beds out with my men. I've heard that black don't rub off. I'd appreciate havin' two of your troopers reinforce my herd guard. Would you mind if we loaned you Winchesters instead of those single shots?"

"Glad to help, Mr. Turner. You know my men aren't cowhands?"

"It's not the cows I worryin' about, it's the Cheyenne."

———

The sleepless night was long and miserable for me. My mind raced and sleep wouldn't come. The presence of twelve extra men brought a sense of security to camp. Seventeen cattle were dead or had to be put down. We butchered as much beef as we could use before it would spoil. After breakfast we headed north.

The next stop was Soldier Springs. A huge lone cottonwood tree stood sentinel along Big Elk Creek. There was an abundance of grass for the livestock. The sergeant and one trooper scouted ahead with me, while the corporal and the rest of the squad brought up the rear behind the drag riders, ready to respond wherever they were needed.

Soldier Springs was beautiful. A small waterfall tumbled down the red sandstone bluff into a crystal clear pool. In spite of the beauty, we set up a defensive perimeter again. However, there was something about the setting that was soothing to the spirit. Kelly cooked steaks, biscuits and beans followed by an apricot cobbler. The fresh beef was a treat for all of us, especially the soldiers.

After supper a trooper approached me. "Sah, I was with Colonel Mackenzie at Palo Duro. There was a scout with him named Noah Turner. He looks a right smart like you, sah."

"That's my brother. I ain't seen or heard from him since '72. How is he?"

"We talked some. He been buffalo huntin' when the Comanche killed his wife. He took up scoutin' for Mackenzie to settle the score."

"Anythin' else you remember?"

"No, sah. Dat's all."

"Thanks, trooper. You ain't half bad for a colored Yankee soldier." I shook his hand and my thoughts drifted to Noah.

We crossed the Washita; the water was down and there wasn't any quicksand. We forted up again that night, still glad for our extra guests. My melancholy was gradually lessening. I knew I had done all anyone could have done. But a certain kernel of guilt for the death of the boys would never leave me.

The trail veered northeast for a ways to avoid alkali water. Another day and a night with the herd brought us to Fort Supply. I hired two out of work buffalo hunters as teamsters. I didn't want to insult them, but I paid for them to visit the local bathhouse and laundry before taking them with us. They took it in stride, looking like new men when they returned scrubbed, shorn, shaved, and in clean clothes. I hardly took the time to learn their names. I knew I was avoiding the possibility of becoming friends with them. It hurt to lose friends, but not people you hardly knew.

There was news at the fort, all of it bad. General Crooke had been routed by the Northern Cheyenne and Sioux at the Battle of the Rose Bud. George Custer, leading part of the Seventh Cavalry had attacked an enormous encampment of Sioux, Cheyenne and Arapaho on the Little Big Horn River in Montana. The Indians fought back with such a fury that they killed Custer and every last man in his command. Our cavalry escort was visibly shaken.

We restocked a few groceries, Kelly's tobacco and plenty of extra cartridges. I saw that there were two good used Winchesters for sale, complete with saddle scabbards and a hundred rounds of ammunition each. I bought them both. I gave one to Sergeant Alexander and the other to the trooper who had known my brother. "These might save your lives some day."

I went to the telegraph office and wired Mrs. Cooper about Tate's death. There was no one to tell about Tanner.

We all visited the saloon that night. I bought a round of drinks for the soldiers and my crew. For the first time since the war, I got drunk.

The trail headed northwest again through some beautiful country. We crossed the North Fork of the Canadian and camped just north of the river. Luke and Levi brought in a spike buck that Kelly and Little Jake turned into a fine supper of chicken fried venison, beans, biscuits and gravy. It was a welcome break from our routine.

We crossed the Cimarron River at a place known as Deep Hole Crossing. The river was wide and mostly shallow except for a deep channel of slow moving water. The mules swam the wagons across without any difficulty. The horse herd and cows followed readily behind the wagons. The north bank of the Cimarron meant we were in Kansas.

A few days later, the cool deep water of the Arkansas spread out before us with Dodge City perched above the flood line on the other side. Buyers rode on horseback or in buggies to meet the herd, inspect the cattle, carry the news and talk price. One buyer presented a business card that showed he was a buyer for Joseph McCoy. I had always done business with Mr. McCoy or one of his agents. I would dance with the one that brought me.

7

August 23, 1876, Dodge City, Kansas
Bright lights, big city

DODGE CITY SAT ON THE Santa Fe Trail just north of the Arkansas River. The Atchison, Topeka and Santa Fe Railroad had built enormous cattle handling pens here to load cattle. They had already shipped tens of thousands of buffalo hides back to eastern markets.

The primary street was Front Street. There were two huge general stores, Chalk Beeson's Long Branch Saloon, George Hoover's Liquor and Cigar Store, Zimmerman's Gun and Hardware Store, and a number of smaller establishments.

The railroad tracks divided Dodge into two distinctly different towns with their own set of rules. North of the tracks, Dodge City was fairly respectable. There were no bawdy houses, none of the rougher sort of saloons. No one was allowed to carry firearms. They were checked in and out at the sheriff's office any time of the day or night. The venerable Dodge House Hotel and Restaurant catered to Dodge's tamer visitors and citizens.

South of the tracks, it was anything goes short of murder or robbery. It was rowdy, loud, exciting and dangerous. There was an ice house that provided that rare commodity to keep the beer uncommonly cold.

There was a bridge across the Arkansas for horses and wagons, but cattle were expected to swim. Our cattle brought thirty-two dollars a head once they were delivered and counted at the pens late that afternoon. We set up camp south of the river in a shady grove of trees.

The agent went with me to the two story brick bank. He presented a draft to the bank manager. I drew out enough coin to pay the men, fill the freight wagons and have plenty of money for the road.

"Who will give me the best price on five loads of buffalo hides?"

The banker gave me a name and directions. "You stand there with a couple of friends while they count those hides. Sometimes he gets a little careless with his counting when nobody's watching."

The cattle buyer gave me a draft made out to a reputable Chinese bath house and laundry north of the tracks. He handed me another for dinner at the Dodge House. "I appreciate your business, Mr. Turner."

I assigned Zach, Tyler, Kirby and Keenan to Kelly's care. They all got along well with Little Jake. I gave Kelly an extra five dollars to spend on treats for the boys.

When we arrived at the Chinese bath house and laundry, the Nixon boys and Little Jake set up quite a howl. They had never seen anything quite like it. Through the rows of curtained partitions I could hear them splashing in the big copper tubs.

"Hey, Kirby! I'm makin' bubbles!"

"Keenan, you just don't have any manners at all, do ya'?"

I enjoyed the long soak in the hot water. The dirt, grime and sweat came off with some stiff scrubbing and the scented lye soap. It seemed like the tension in my shoulders and neck slowly eased away.

The little Chinese lady who gave me the the haircut and shave was older than the hills, but she sure did a good job. They finally delivered my cleaned and pressed clothes, well brushed hat and nicely shined boots. We regrouped on the front porch.

"That's the first bath I ever took in a real bathtub." Tyler bragged.

"We got a big wash tub at Fort Griffin we got to stand up in to take a bath." Kirby explained.

"Yeah, and I came sneakin' up behind and got you with a bucket of cold well water!"

"Sometimes I don't know why Momma didn't drown you when you was borned."

"Come on boys. It's lunch on Mr. McCoy at the Dodge House."

The waiter brought baskets full of hot yeast rolls and bowls of fresh butter, platters of fried chicken, mashed potatoes and gravy, and corn-fed beefsteaks. There was plenty of good strong coffee, chocolate cake and ice cream for dessert.

I passed around everybody's pay, warned them not to spend it all, and told everyone except Pecos and Matt they had to stay north of the railroad tracks. Kelly took off towing the youngsters. The freighters I had hired at Fort Supply had taken their pay and disappeared. The rest of us drove the five loads of hides to the buyer. He offered what I expected and I stood watching him count the hides.

"What's a matter, don't you trust me?"

"Don't know ya' well enough to say I do or I don't."

He wrote a draft which I took to the bank and cashed into gold and silver coins. The two sisters would share almost three thousand dollars, but it had cost them the lives of their husbands and one son. I doubted it was worth it.

I drifted along Front Street. I saw the younger set run by in new boots and hats. I was intrigued by the Liquor and Tobacco Store. When I walked in, the aroma was intoxicating.

"Can I help you with something, sir?"

"What's that good smell?"

"I believe you are enjoying the aroma of our selection of fine tobaccos. Would you like to show you some you might like?"

He opened jar after fragrant jar of various types and blends of tobacco. There was one blend that smelled like good dark tobacco with a hint of vanilla, fine whiskey, and brown sugar. "That's our own house blend number seven. It's one of our best sellers. It has some good dark burley and some Virginia Cavendish. It is aged in a tobacco press for a year and allowed to ferment. That's what gives it such an interesting taste and aroma. Would you like to try it?"

"I don't smoke, and I hardly ever chew. I wouldn't know what to do with it."

"Let me fix you a small sample pipe to try. It's free." He carefully packed the black tobacco flakes into a long-stem clay pipe. He lit it and got it going good, then handed it to me. "Now, don't inhale."

I sat down near the counter and drew on the pipe. My mouth was filled with the intense taste and aroma of the tobacco. I puffed slowly, enjoying it immensely. I felt the top of my head feel warm like a wool cap. My body felt relaxed and my mind felt at ease. "Say, I like this. Would you fix me up with a starter set and a year's worth of tobacco?"

"The tobacco keeps a long time in an unopened tin. I'll get you all fixed up with a good briar pipe and a pipe tool for cleaning it."

I walked out of the store with a cloth sack holding my new pipe and what I hoped would be about a year's worth of tobacco. Having never used it before, the clerk had helped me make a rough guess.

I bought two new pairs of Levi's, two shirts, a new pair of boots, plus a store made dress for Mother and one for Alice. I had lists of things they needed and wanted and did my best to get them all. I made sure to get the things they had ordered at Fort Supply, Fort Griffin, and the store at Belle Plain. We filled the bottoms of the wagons with sawed cured lumber and sheet metal, kegs of nails and boxes of hand tools. There were barrels of molasses, sacks of flour and cornmeal, kegs of vinegar, cases of whiskey, sacks of salt and cans of spices, tomatoes, peaches, sardines and evaporated milk. There were cases of enamelware, pots, pans and skillets. There were cases of various kinds of cartridges loaded next to green coffee beans and cases of roasted Arbuckle's coffee. Bolts of cloth of every kind, sacks of candy and medicines filled out the load.

I found Kelly and the boys, interrupting their adventures long enough to help me drive the wagons back to camp. I had them put the wagon bows up and stretch on the wagon canvas. This cargo needed to stay dry.

We ate at a chili joint with the younger boys, then had a drink with Luke, Levi, Kyle and Jake. They were having fun, but not enough to get in trouble. The horses Matt and Pecos had been riding were tied in front of a saloon south of the tracks. I walked down just to check in on them. They were in a mostly friendly low stakes poker game with some recently washed buffalo hunters. The prettiest girls in the place clustered around those two Texas drovers. It looked like they were doing fine.

"See y'all in the mornin'. We got horses and mules to shoe."

"Good night, boss. See ya in the mornin'!"

I rode back to camp to find everyone else already in for the night. We weren't a very lively crew. I leaned back against a wagon wheel, lit up my new pipe and enjoyed the smoke writhing around me. When it was done, I knocked out the cold ashes, and fell asleep right where I was sitting and dreamed of Texas.

8

August 25, 1876, south bank of the Arkansas River, Kansas
Headed home to Texas

PECOS AND MATT WERE
back at camp for breakfast, but just couldn't face anything but
black coffee. "Boys, the grease is still hot. Why don't ya let me
fry ya up some nice eggs?" Both turned a sickly color of green.
"If ya don't want eggs, I bought some canned sardines." At
Kelly's cruel teasing, they both headed for the bushes.

"Have a good time, did ya, Matt?"

"I don't remember if I did or not, Biscuit."

"Did we have a good time, Pecos?"

"I feel like I been hit in the head with a skillet."

"You two better get to shoein' them horses and mules."

"Dang, Aaron."

"Dang nothin'! You better get to workin'!"

The rest of us checked and adjusted harness, greased
the wagon axles, and evened out their loads. Kelly cooked
an especially spicy and greasy batch of chili for lunch. The
boys took turns squatting down near Pecos or Matt so they
could smell and see it. The younger ones spent the afternoon
swimming or fishing in the Arkansas. They caught enough
catfish for a big supper. Ol' Biscuit outdid himself with the
catfish fried in cornmeal, hush puppies, boiled yellow squash

and a huge blackberry cobbler. Nobody went back into Dodge that night. It seems everybody was just about partied out.

—————

"Hup, mules!" The long black whip cracked sharply over the broad backs of the mules. All six wagons lurched forward. Luke and Levi had become teamsters for the return trip. Little Jake and the rest of us on horseback got the remuda moving. The stock was fresh and rested. We made better than twenty miles south the first day.

When we arrived at the Deep Hole Crossing on the Cimarron River, the water was running fast and full of floating debris. We camped north of the river two days and nights waiting for the water to go down so that we could leave Kansas behind. I was anxious to get moving, but the river had only receded modestly.

"Kelly, I know the horses can get across pretty easy now, but the water's too fast for the mules to drag the wagons across. We're gonna swim the mules over, hitch 'em together, and tow the wagons to the other side." Everybody stripped down to their summer drawers and unsaddled their horses, stowing everything in the chuck wagon.

All six teams were driven across, still wearing harness and dragging a thick manila rope. The best mules were double teamed. There would be eight head pulling on the rope. Kelly fastened it to the tongue of the chuck wagon and another to the rear of the wagon. He looped the rope around the trunk of a smooth cottonwood and fastened to the saddle horn of Kelly's enormous draft horse.

"Little Jake, if the rear of that wagon gets swingin' too far down stream, you and Ol' Thunder pull 'til its straight. Let's go!"

Kyle led the eight mules slowly away from the river until the slack was pulled out of the rope. The wagon began to inch forward into the swirling water. "Now, Kyle!"

"Hup, mules!" Kyle pulled on the left mule's headstall until they were all in a slow trot. The chuck wagon surged into the muddy water. The current started to swing the rear downstream.

"Git up, Thunder!" The big horse continued to pull until the wagon was straight. They were across.

The process was repeated with the other five wagons until they were all safely across. Even though we were tired, we pushed on to get ten miles behind us before stopping for the day.

A full day's travel took us across the North Canadian River and on south to Fort Supply. Our soldier friends were in camp, so we met them at the tavern and bought the first round. The storekeeper bought a whole wagon load of supplies. He didn't even blink when I charged twice what I'd paid in Dodge. We redistributed the goods from the other wagons to even out the loads.

Kelly bought some fresh vegetables, milk and eggs, plus a little surprise.

"Boys, I bought us a cured ham, sweet taters, roastin' ears and a whole sack of tomaters. We're gonna have us a feast!"

Jake tuned his fiddle and Matt got down his guitar after supper. I leaned against a wagon wheel, enjoying the music and my pipe.

Zach was the first one up the next morning. "I swear to goodness, Kelly is cookin' ham steaks, biscuits, red eye gravy and fried eggs!" It was a good start to the day.

Sergeant Alexander and his troopers escorted us down the trail. I noticed that all the soldiers carried Winchesters now. They scouted ahead and all around us, but were always close enough to hear a gunshot.

Even though they brought their own rations, Biscuit fixed supper for the soldiers every evening. Since we were back in Cheyenne country, we forted up the wagons at night. Nobody seemed uncomfortable around the black troopers. They were men just doing a job and trying to stay alive like the rest of us. We were mighty glad for the company and extra guns.

We camped at Soldier Springs with its single huge cottonwood tree and tumbling waterfall on Big Elk Creek. It was a deceptively beautiful, dangerous place.

"Aaron, you know where our next stop is, don't ya?"

"Yeah, Pecos. I can get that place out of my head. I wish there was some way around it, but there's not."

"You think them colored troopers is gonna do us any good if them Cheyenne come back?"

"Heck, yeah, I do. I've watched 'em. They know their business."

"The only time I remember seein' any of 'em fight was at Nashville. They weren't too scary."

"They ran our skinny butts all the way outta Tennessee didn't they? Would you feel safer without 'em?"

Pecos pulled off his hat and ran his hand through his hair. "I git your point."

———

Comanche Springs on Big Elk Creek, the sight of it made my skin crawl. The two graves lay undisturbed near the clear bubbling water in the shadow of the red sandstone bluffs. My mouth went dry and my stomach drew up into a tight knot. No matter what anyone said, I still felt the death of the two boys had been my fault.

We forted up the wagons exactly where we had in July. Tyler, Kirby and Keenan paid their respects at the graves. Little Jake and Zach spent half an hour gathering up forgotten brass shell casings. It had been one hell of a fight. The wild animals had scattered the bones of the dead cattle we had left in the lush meadows. They were a reminder of the mortal nature of our desperate defense.

That night after supper, Matt and Jake played "Shall We Gather at the River" and sang along quietly. Even the soldiers were touched. They continued to play one hymn after another until, one by one, the camp was asleep. I had been moved by the songs and sat alone smoking my pipe thinking about my life and all that I had seen and done. I had killed my first man at thirteen in the war and would never forget it, but there had been many more after that. I had seen things that had left me changed inside, hardened somehow, and old beyond my years. I didn't feel guilty about those things. That had been war. But I felt guilty for the deaths of Tanner Beasley and Tate Cooper. As I sat and smoked, I came to realize that since I had come home from the war, I had taken on being responsible for everybody. Momma had told me I wasn't responsible to anyone but God, and only for my own actions. Maybe so, but I didn't have it figured out yet. I sat awake all night and watched the stars come out. And I prayed. I prayed for the first time in years.

———

The soldiers left us at the crossing of the North Fork of the Red River. As hard as it was for me to imagine, we had become friends: Billy Yank with Johnny Reb, black with white.

Soon, we splashed across the Red River at Doan's Crossing back into Texas. "Mr. Doan, I got a load of trade goods for ya. I hope I got everything ya wanted."

"Well, let's see what ya got. Yes, I durn sure could use this stuff." He bought two whole wagon loads, again at twice what I had paid in Dodge. "You know, son, I have had to pay a lot more than what you're chargin' for most of this stuff."

"No sir, I didn't. I charged twice what it cost me. You think that's fair?"

"It's more than fair to me."

"I never been a trader. I just figured I could make a little extra money on the trip haulin' hides to Dodge and bringin' back things that folks could use around here." We visited quite a while and caught up on the news. There was a fairly fresh newspaper on the bar.

"Aaron, listen to this!" Kyle read out loud to us. "The notorious James and Coulter gang got a dose of their own medicine when they attempted to rob a bank in Northfield, Minnesota. Armed citizens realized a robbery was in progress and severely mauled the gang. Several gang members were left dead or wounded in the streets and no money was taken. The citizens suffered only minor injuries."

"What goes around, comes around. Mr. Doan, the James gang tried to rob us back in '66. One of our men was in the woods with a Henry repeatin' rifle. He killed ol' Jesse's horse dead right out from under him! Kyle here saddled him up another horse before they rode off."

"Who shot the horse?"

We exchanged glances. "It was a friend of ours that got killed by the Kiowa."

"I'd like to shake his hand."

Pecos stood up, heading for the door muttering "Oh, no, you wouldn't."

"There's the Pease River, Keenan. You thirsty?"

"Oh, shut up, Kirby!"

We passed through the small towns of Seymour and Throckmorton before arriving at Fort Griffin. Keenan and Kirby set the brakes on their wagons and took off running to see their mother, aunt and cousin. There was plenty of crying on the front porch, even for those two tough women.

"Mrs. Cooper, I'm so sorry about Tate. I told you in the telegram, he fought like a wild cat, but the Cheyenne got up behind him. He never had a chance. I brung ya his pay, just like he made the whole trip. We got all his belongings in this sack except the rifle. It's at the bottom of that creek somewhere."

"Thank ya for sendin' the telegram. The boys said he got buried proper."

"Yes ma'am. Prayed and sang over, too."

"Mrs. Nixon, if you'll give me back my bank draft, I'll swap ya for coin, plus I got the money for the hides. They sold good. I subtracted the money for the supplies from the hide money at Dodge City prices. I hauled for free."

"Thanks, Aaron. That's more than fair."

Tyler Beasley looked around forlornly. There was no one to greet him. The only family he had left was the brother we buried at Comanche Springs. "Aaron, you reckon I could come work for you? I ain't got any family and nowhere to go. I'll learn fast and work hard."

"What do you think about us roundin' up a stray, Pecos? He ain't worth much, but he don't eat much neither."

"He'll do. But don't let him drive the wagon across any flooded rivers. He might drown our good mules and cost us a wagon, too."

"Tyler, it's a deal. Now I aim to work you as hard as me and Pecos work, but I'll pay you the same money and give you room and board. You give me any trouble, I'll send you back here."

We all ate supper at the "Sisters' Mercantile, Tavern and Inn." It was real good, nearly as good as Kelly's cooking. We sent word to the fort and met Sergeant O'Malley and his squad at the Bull's Head Saloon. As I had promised, the first drink was on me. We swapped lies for a while and listened to their sad tale of walking back to Fort Griffin, like a bunch of old friends. We laughed at the lickin' we had given them with the axe handles. O'Malley had me call out like I was a Yankee captain again.

"We couldn't have told the truth; nobody would have believed us!"

I never would have thought that at the trails end I'd have two Blue-belly sergeants and two squads of colored soldiers for friends. Things had changed a lot in the last few years.

9

December 25, 1876, Groesbeck, Limestone County, Texas
Home for Christmas

THE SCENT OF FRESH coffee and frying bacon floated up the worn oak stairs to the room that had been mine all my life. But, the house wasn't in Leon County any more. We had moved it and reassembled it at Groesbeck in Limestone County after trouble with the Klan. The other bed in the room, the one where my brother Noah had always slept, was empty. In a few months, it would be four years since we had seen or heard from him. The soldier I had met had seen him scouting for Mackenzie in '74. I had heard Colonel Mackenzie's unit had been transferred from Texas to Nebraska to mop up some Indian problems there. He had defeated Chief Dull Knife of the Northern Cheyenne in a pitched battle on the Powder River in the Wyoming Territory. I wondered if he had been there as a scout.

Pecos was still asleep across the hall, and I hadn't heard Alice get up yet. I dressed and went downstairs to have some quiet time with Mother.

"Mornin' sunshine! How'd you sleep?"

I gave Momma a kiss on the cheek and a nice hug. "I slept good, Momma. It's good to be home. Oh, Merry Christmas!"

"Same to you, son. Coffee?"

"Yessum. Thanks."

We talked of many things as we shared our coffee and our thoughts. I told her about the drive, the Cheyenne raid, the two boys, everything. She grew quiet. "Aaron, since you were ten years old, you've been carrying the world on your shoulders. I remember how you used to try to fight sorry ol' Lige Campbell when he mistreated me. I wish I had never met that good-for-nothing evil drunkard. After the war, you sort of naturally became the boss of the cattle operation, in spite of you being the youngest. You have always amazed me, son. Sometimes I worry you're mighty hard on yourself. No one is perfect, Aaron. Your father used to say 'None are perfect but by the blood of the blessed Lamb of God.' Oh, that reminds me, there is a circuit riding Methodist preacher holding Christmas night services at six o'clock. Would go with me?"

"I'd love to, Momma. Maybe that ol' heathen Pecos will go with us."

Christmas lunch was especially good. My sister, Mary Ann, and her husband Pinckney Hawkins were there, as was my half-brother, Marcus, and his wife, Glynna. Mary Ann was my full sister. Marcus was a King. His father had died before my father met Mother. My father had died when I was only a year old and I didn't remember a thing about him. Pecos was there, as was my niece, Alice. Tyler Beasley had been invited to stay with the Webb's at Belle Plain for Christmas. I had agreed as long as he rode over to check the stock every day. I still had one foot in Groesbeck and one in Callahan County. We had tripled the length and doubled the width of our dugout at the ranch to accommodate storage for our extra supplies. We had even built bunk bed with lumber and rawhide strips.

We all cleaned up and went down to the little community church building there in Groesbeck. It was the Methodists' turn to use it. The preacher was a young man, not much older than me. He told how the "Law of Sin and Death" separates man from God. But God had allowed His own Son to pay the price for the sins of all men. Any that would call upon Jesus, confess their sins and be baptized would be saved. He went on to explain that not only would a man be saved, but that God would adopt him as his own child.

Something stirred deep within me. I felt separated from God and longed to have my sins washed away through Jesus' blood. When he gave the altar call and the singing began, I was trembling ever so slightly all over. I gripped the back of the pew in front of me. The preacher stopped the singing for a minute.

"I know that there are some who are aching to know their Father, to be drawn to His side, to be forgiven of their sins, to become a child of God. The congregation began singing 'Softly and Tenderly Jesus is Calling.'"

I turned loose of the pew and walked to the front and sat down. The preacher talked to me and I let him know I was ready to be saved.

The small assembly gathered around me as I knelt while the preacher prayed for me. "Aaron, because of your confession that Jesus is the Son of God, I baptize you in the name of the Father, the Son and the Holy Spirit." He poured water on my head from a white pitcher that ran down and mingled with the tears on my face. Everyone gathered closer as the preacher said another prayer. As he was finished, there were hugs and handshakes all around. Momma and Mary Ann cried and hugged me. Women I didn't know came up and hugged me. Even Alice came up and gave me a half-hearted hug like I might be contaminated with some disease. Marcus and Pink shook hands and said they were proud of me, as did some men I didn't know.

Pecos kind of stood back until the crowd was gone, then walked up and started to shake my hand. But he grabbed me around the shoulders in a bear hug. "You're the best friend I got in the world. I'm mighty proud of you, amigo." The rascal had tears in his eyes. I felt better than I ever remembered feeling in my life.

Mother came back and motioned for me to sit down next to her on the front pew. "Aaron, you didn't know your daddy, but he was a good man. You remember being told he was a Methodist preacher. Well, he was a lot more than that to a lot of people. I just want you to know that he would be very proud of you." She paused. "He would be proud of you for the man you have become, how you try to take care of everybody, including me. Lord, son. I know I'm awful proud of you myself."

An invitation arrived to a New Year's Eve dance in the home of George and Elizabeth Fisher. All of us cleaned up to go, even Alice. Pecos never missed a party.

We took a buggy and a couple of horses. The night was crisp and clear. The horses' breath left great clouds of steam in the cold still air. The moon had already set, so the stars were especially bright. We arrived to find a good crowd already in the party spirit. The big house was warm and filled with the scent of desserts. A beautiful young woman greeted my mother and Alice.

"I'm Ella, George and Elizabeth's daughter. I know who you are, but haven't met you. I'm glad you could come."

"I'm Aaron Turner. This is my friend, Pecos Wade."

"I know who you are, Aaron. I was at church on Christmas. May I take your hats and coats?"

"Thank you, Miss Ella." Pecos and I exchanged grins.

A good fiddler and guitar player were tuning up. They lit into "Ol' Joe Clark" as well as I had ever heard it played. Ella happened to be standing near us when the music started.

I hesitated for a second, but after an elbow from Pecos, I asked her if she would like to dance.

"Yes, thanks for asking."

That began a wonderful evening of dancing, laughter, talking and eating. I danced almost every dance with her except a waltz with Momma. She also made me dance once with Alice. I swear she was deliberately stepping on my toes. The musicians finally played "Auld Lang Syne" at midnight. Mr. Fisher, who was rumored to be something of a character, thanked everyone for coming. Ella grabbed my hand. "Would you ask my father if you could call on me?"

"I sure would!"

"Mrs. Fisher, Mr. Fisher. I'm Aaron Turner, Nancy Turner's son. Thank you for inviting me."

"You're the young man who got baptized on Christmas Day."

"Yes ma'am. Mr. Fisher, I'd like to ask if I could call on Ella?"

"What do ya wanna call her? Ya already know her name."

"No, I mean I'd like to see her."

"Is there somethin' the matter with your eyes, boy? I can see her just fine."

Ella moved in front of her grinning father and politely stepped squarely on his toes. "Girl, are you tryin' to kill me?"

"It's alright, Daddy. You've got extra toes. I believe my father was just about to say you would be welcome to call on me any time."

"Oh, whatever she says is alright with me. I couldn't win an argument with either of these women with three lawyers and a paid off judge. Yes, you can call on her and see her, too. Now, goodnight, young gentleman."

I saw Ella often that winter at Groesbeck. Pecos and I got invited for Sunday lunch several times. I finally got brave enough to pick her up for a buggy ride on a pretty day. I had never taken the time for showing much interest in girls, but that was changing fast.

When it came time to move back to our cow camp in Callahan County for the spring, I gave Ella the address of the little post office at Belle Plain. She made me promise to write her in Limestone County.

Before we left, a letter arrived from Fort Robinson, Nebraska

Dear Mother, Aaron and all,

I am writing to tell you I am alive and well. I hunted buffalo along the Republican River, down into Kansas along the Arkansas, and finally, on the High Plains of Texas along the Canadian River. The Comanche raided our camp and killed my wife, Mary. I know you just met her at the wedding, but she was a good woman. I took my wagons, mules and hides to Adobe Walls to sell out the whole business. We got caught in a three day Indian fight, but finally drove them away. I was sick of the hide business and wanted revenge on the Comanche, so I signed up as a scout for Colonel Ranald Mackenzie. I didn't have to wear blue, but my paycheck came from the United States Army. Things sure have changed. We caught the Comanche in their winter camp down in

Palo Duro Canyon and scattered them pretty good. Mainly, we captured their horse herd. We killed all fourteen hundred head. It made me sick, but even the Comanche can't steal a dead horse. After Quannah Parker took his Nocona band in to the reservation at Fort Sill, Mackenzie got us transferred to Fort Robinson to fight Cheyenne, Arapaho and Sioux. We have our hands full, but the Colonel knows his business. I do not know when I will be back in Texas. I have a sizable amount of money at the Businessman's Bank of Omaha under both my name and Aaron's. If something should happen to me, Aaron, please use the money to make sure Mother is well situated and the rest is to use as you see fit. I hope to see you if I am able. There is no excuse for not contacting you. Please forgive me. I have been preoccupied with my own problems, but you are always in my heart.

Love, your son and brother,

Noah

10

May 1, 1877, Turner Ranch, Callahan County, Texas
Lost and Found

        "LOOK OUT! THAT OL' lineback's gonna git in your pocket!"

Jake heard his brother's warning and spurred the horse out of the way. The old cross-bred cow stood bellowing, shaking her head, slinging snot and pawing dirt over her back.

"Boys, that's the last one. We got 'em all sorted. I'm glad that witch is headed for Kansas. I don't like her attitude. She's meaner than Alice! Biscuit, how's supper comin', you ol' bald headed giant?"

"Pecos, you're gonna get salt in your coffee if you don't shut your trap. Come and git it before I throw it out!"

Little Jake served up plates of beans, bacon and cornbread. Everybody went back for second and third helpings. It had been a long hard day.

"How many on the tally book, Pecos?"

"Four hundred and ninety-seven, all home raised cattle."

The next morning we drove the freight wagons, remuda and cattle over Lytle's Gap to Belle Plain. We turned our stock into Captain Tyus' fenced pasture.

"Hello, Cap. You got yours ready for the trail?"

"Eight hundred and three head of good market ready cattle."

"It's gonna be our biggest herd yet, and there ain't a maverick in the bunch. I sure don't miss the old days. That was too much like work. Pecos got all our ridin' stock and mules shod. Is Matt finished with yours?"

"Yes, we're good to go for the mornin'."

————————

Herds of cattle that have been together any length of time know their own and have worked out their own pecking order. These cattle were strangers. All night long they bawled and milled about getting acquainted and establishing dominance. It would take a couple of weeks to get all straightened out. They were still pushing and shoving at daylight.

With a good breakfast under our belts, we were ready for the road. The chuck wagon always took the lead, followed by the five freight wagons, the remuda, then the herd. We pushed the six miles to Clyde, then another five to make sure the cattle were a little tired their first night on the trail. I had hired a couple of students from Belle Plain College to drive wagons for me as far as Fort Griffin where we would pick up the Nixon boys. They had tied their horses on behind the wagon for the trip back.

I bought five loads of good hides plenty cheap. They would bring triple the price in Dodge City, but the trick was to get them there. We made our camp on the Clear Fork of the Brazos just east of town. The Nixon boys had been expecting us and had ridden out to meet the herd. They were both a little taller and had even more freckles.

"Howdy, boys! How are the Nixon knot heads? Been drinkin' any more gyp water, Keenan?"

"Boss, I ain't even got my gear in the wagon and you're already pickin' on me. Come on up to the tavern about seven. Momma said come hungry."

Mrs. Nixon, Mrs. Cooper and Tory hadn't changed any that I could tell. There wasn't anybody in Fort Griffin, black, red or white, they couldn't handle, except those two red-headed boys. It took a little beating to keep them half-way in line. Robin gave me their list of things to buy in Dodge, and said they were going to pay the delivered price this year, instead of the discount I gave them last year. I didn't argue. We were all trying to make an honest dollar.

Sergeant O'Malley and his troopers came down from the fort after supper. They insisted it was their turn to buy the first round as long as we didn't bring any axe handles.

We had been telling tall tales for half an hour before I noticed that Keenan had slipped in unnoticed and had helped himself freely to the adult beverages.

"Hey, Bosh, there's two of ya!"

We carried him outside on the porch where he promptly fell asleep snoring. I hoped his Momma didn't catch him, or she'd have the hide off the little weasel.

O'Malley took on a more serious tone. "Aaron, Chief Sitting Bull and the whole Lakota tribe slipped across the line into Canada. Crazy Horse took his people into Fort Robinson. Whether he done it or not, I don't know, but they claim he attacked a guard and was shot to death trying to escape. It sounds a bit too tidy to me. The war on the Northern Plains is about over."

A man at the bar told us that several ranches had started up on the southern Plains now that the Comanche were gone. "Charles Goodnight has a big ranch down in Palo Duro Canyon. The Matador Ranch is running on range down around the Pease River country, and the Spur Ranch was a ways south of that."

I turned to Pecos. "Maybe Noah will come home now that all the buffalo are dead and the Indians gone. There's nothin' left to kill."

_____

We sent the college boys home and hired a couple of out of work buffalo skinners to drive the wagons to Dodge. "No drinkin' unless me or the cook offers it, and no gamblin' for money on the drive. I know the buffalo huntin' days around here are over. Pay's a dollar a day plus keep. You can take it or leave it. If you hire on, I'm payin' to git both of you washed, shaved and cleaned up before we leave." Having no other options, they agreed.

We crossed the Pease near Vernon and bedded the cattle down about five miles south of Doan's Crossing. The weather had been unsettled, hot and humid all day. A line of tall dark clouds had dogged our path to the west all day. The west wind carried the scent of a storm. Kelly was just putting away the supper dishes when flickers of lightning appeared in the distance. The time it took us to hear the thunder indicated the storm was closer than it looked. Forked lightning jumped from cloud to cloud, and sometimes straight to the ground. It was moving fast now. An icy cold wind swept down from the front of the towering thunderheads. Lightning now flashed all around us with the thunder coming simultaneously. A monster storm was right on top of us.

"All hands and the cook!"

Everyone grabbed a picketed horse, including Little Jake, Kelly and all the teamsters. Pecos took half the men to the east of the herd and Matt took the other half around to the west. The cattle were on their feet and milling nervously when the sky exploded like an artillery duel. The cattle bawled and took off running. Some of the less experienced men crowded too close, causing the cattle to split off into smaller bunches. We had to keep them together! Rather than stop and let them regroup, they tried to chase them back, succeeding in only scattering them worse.

In frustration, I reined up near Pecos. "I shoulda shot them greenhorns or left 'em on the wagons. We got cattle scattered seven ways to Sunday. There's enough light left, maybe we can push 'em back into one herd. Put them teamsters back to tend to the wagons and mules. The rest of us will split up and ease 'em back together. If I see anybody chousin' 'em, I'm gonna beat 'em with my chaps!"

"Pecos, if I get separated, you're in charge. Keep headin' 'em north. Stop at Doan's Store and check for news. If any of us get lost, that would be a good meetin' place. Matt, you know if something happens to both me and Pecos, you're in charge. Of all the storms and stampedes we've had with wilder cattle than these, this is the biggest mess I ever saw!"

I was riding my favorite cow horse, a line back red dun mare called "Moon" because of a small quarter-moon mark on her forehead. I had raised her grandma, her momma and her daddy. I had been there the day she was born and had trained her myself. She and I went together like a glove and a hand. She was tough and could take a lot of hard riding, plus she was about the best cow horse I had ever owned. She could spin on a dime and give you back nine cents change. There wasn't a bull too big for her to drag or a calf too small to rope. Moon could follow a specific animal all through a herd and cut her out. She knew when to step in and when to ease back. She could do everything except speak Spanish, and she understood that.

I saw a bunch of about twenty straight longhorn steers one of the neighbors had added to the herd. They slipped over a rise and disappeared into the cedars. By the time I topped the ridge, I caught a glimpse of some tails heading northeast deeper into the brush. This bunch had been a headache since the first day from Belle Plain on north. I was afraid they might turn back south and head for Callahan County. I wouldn't much care if they did, but in all the time I had been doing this, I had never lost any cattle to straying, and I didn't intend to start now.

The storm had slowed to a steady rain, but a crash of lightning revealed the clouds were tall as mountains with rolled under edges and a sickly green color. I had lived in Texas all my life and knew trouble when I saw it. Fat, cold raindrops began to fall. They made a nice splash as they hit the soaked ground. Lightning continued to flash in every direction. I stepped off of Moon to make less of a target and found very little shelter under a small rocky overhang. The rain fell faster and faster until it was falling in sheets. Pea-sized hail mixed with the rain until the ground was white. The size of the hail quickly increased until it was as big as eggs.

The wind whirled in every direction, blowing rain under the rocky ledge and forcing water beneath my yellow slicker. In minutes, I was soaked to the bone. The rain continued to pour down, floating the hail away with it. Nearby, a small stream was roaring.

As the storm drifted east, the sky cleared enough to the west to show a soggy sunset. I tried to cut the tracks of the steers, but the storm had washed them away. The wind shifted briefly and Moon snorted, stomped her foot and pointed her ears north. I climbed back on and let her have her head. She worked her way around cedars and brush until a grassy clearing of slightly higher ground appeared. In the middle of it were the still smoldering bodies of three longhorn steers. They were twisted into unnatural shapes, the tips of their horns were burnt black and their hooves had been blown off. The smell of burned hair and flesh was sickening and strong.

Muddy tracks headed off to the northeast. From the distance between the hoof prints, it looked like those cattle were flat covering some ground.

"Moon, I bet the lightnin' that fried their buddies put the fear in 'em."

Darkness was falling fast due to the heavy cloud cover. Those seventeen steers would bring my neighbor a lot of money in Dodge, but I couldn't catch up to them in the dark. Then a chilling observation hit me. There was a real good chance I couldn't find my way back to the herd in the dark either. Those longhorns might be anywhere. They could have turned south and run for the Pease or crashed on past Doan's Store and right across the Red River. I would have to hunker down and wait for morning.

The clearing was a little higher than the ground around it and possessed a very thick covering of buffalo grass. It wasn't muddy like the bare ground and low spots all around me. There was a dead cedar that still had dry brown needles on the brittle branches. I broke off an armload of branches and gathered up some more dead wood in the area. I had some old newspaper in my saddle bags for "necessary" purposes and sulphur matches in a water-proof container. The dry newspaper flared and quickly dried and ignited the dead cedar needles. Small pieces of dead wood and then gradually larger branches were added to the fire until it crackled with warmth, heat and light. It sure felt good.

Propping some larger branches around one side of the fire, I hung out my wet clothes to dry and placed my boots near enough that they slowly began to steam. I had to turn everything occasionally to keep it drying evenly.

Here I sat on my heels, buck naked, watching the fire. There is something about being lost in the brush in your birthday suit within arrow shot of Indian Territory that makes a fellow feel pretty vulnerable.

I kept my Winchester and Colt near to hand. It must be some spectacle for a Texas trail boss to be in my predicament; at least Moon wasn't going to tell anyone. I put hobbles on her and fastened her lead rope to a picket stake I pushed into the ground so she could graze a little on the thick buffalo grass. Her saddle was soaked, as was the wool blanket. They completed the semi-circle of slowly drying, steaming items around the fire.

The rumbling in my stomach reminded me I hadn't eaten since breakfast. There had been some cornbread wrapped in a rag in my saddle bags and some left-over bacon. As I opened the cloth, I found a double handful of cornmeal mush. I greedily ate it. I had eaten worse things during the war. The bacon was limp, but edible. I had busted my rear all day, and this hardly put a dent in my appetite. I had eaten plenty of horsemeat in my day, but Moon was safe for now. However, the carcasses of the lightning killed steers offered some promise for scavenging; I had learned to be an expert at scavenging usable meat from battle killed horses and mules. And there was at least one fondly remembered instance when Pecos, Noah and I had "scavenged" some live hogs from a prosperous Confederate farmer at Tuscumbia, Alabama. Our whole company ate well for three days.

My naked, skinny six foot four frame stepped gingerly on bare feet to the dead steers. I took my sheath knife and butchered out the back straps from all three steers. When I returned to the fire, I sliced off some steaks that I skewered on green sticks and stuck them in the ground near the fire. I kept them turning to cook evenly. The sizzling meat and the aroma of roasting beef were more than I could stand. I ate the first steak while it was still a little bloody in the middle. The meat was tough as an old boot. I chewed and chewed to get it down. A little salt would have gone a long way to making it better, but I was glad for what I had. I did have to wonder if this steer had just dropped dead of old age rather than lightning. The other cuts were cooked a little better, but didn't rate any higher as good groceries. I managed to choke down all of it.

As I groused about the toughness of the last bite, I remembered how lucky I was not to have been struck by lightning, not to have Moon killed or crippled, and how lucky I was to have anything to eat. I felt a little guilty and said a prayer thanking God for sparing me and for providing food for me in the middle of nowhere. I asked Him to help me not be so ungrateful.

I sliced the rest of the meat as thin as I could and draped it over green branches near the fire to slowly dry into something resembling jerky. My drawers had dried, so I felt more dignified as I sat near the fire turning the meat. Soon, I had a shirt, then britches, and finally some socks to wear. The boots, saddle and blanket would be a while getting dry. I wished I had my pipe, but it was rolled up with my tobacco tin in my war bag in the chuck wagon, where ever it might be. I had not seen the glow of any campfire against the cloudy sky or heard a single human sound.

I dragged the saddle to the side and laid out my slicker on the ground. I leaned back to nap, waking occasionally to turn the meat. A gentle nuzzle to my face woke me with a start from a deep sleep. It was full daylight. Moon had pulled her picket stake from the soft ground and come to check on the boss. I slipped on my nearly dry boots and led her to the little arroyo that gurgled near us. She drank all she could hold. The water there had run off from thick grassy ground and had just a tinge of red to it. I drank all I wanted, then filled my canteen.

"Girl, this blanket's still damp. I'm sorry about that." I finished saddling her, and stuffed the reasonably dry jerky in the rag from my saddle bag. I rolled up my slicker and tied it behind the cantle, holstered my Colt and slipped the Winchester in the rifle boot. The last time I'd seen the steers, they were heading northeast, so Moon and I headed that way.

Within a mile or so, Moon nickered and pointed her ears. I listened, too. I could faintly hear large animals moving in the brush. I gave Moon her head and she eased toward the sound. The brush opened into a grassy prairie of maybe forty acres of good native grass. The longhorns I was trailing were grazing with a set of really nice cross-bred cattle. Cattle this nice hadn't strayed, there had to be someone living close by.

We eased on about two miles to the east and found a clearing of several acres with a small cabin, corral and outbuildings. Moon stamped her foot nervously. I felt it, too. Something wasn't right. My skin prickled all over. I slipped the rifle out and laid it across my lap as we slowly rode around the outside of the clearing.

Moon stopped dead in her tracks. Her ears pointed straight at the cabin. Then I saw what bothered her and my blood ran cold. The body of an old man lay face down in the dirt with an arrow in his back!

I watched and waited. Chickens scratched around the cabin and a milk cow peered from under a shed. Nothing seemed to be bothering them. I made one more slow circle around the clearing before riding in toward the body.

My hands shook and my mouth went dry as I stepped off Moon and walked cautiously toward the old man, my rifle in my hands. I saw fresh blood oozing from the wound. Dead men don't bleed! This old man was alive, and whoever had tried to kill him couldn't be too far away.

11

Late May, 1877, Northwest Texas Frontier
Chance

"COME ON OL' TIMER. LET'S get you inside the cabin." Moon was tied to the porch and my rifle was next to the door. The gravely wounded man had long flowing white hair and a long untrimmed white beard. He was dressed in buckskin shirt and pants. The deep lines etched in his darkly tanned face spoke of a life outdoors. It was hard to say, but I guessed he might be eighty.

I eased him down on his side on the corn shuck mattress of an old fashioned rawhide-strung bed with the shaft of the arrow facing me. I propped him up on a pillow to keep him from rolling over. His breath was shallow and his pulse weak. Dread came over me as I realized what needed to be done.

My rifle was still by the door. Grabbing it, I led Moon into the rail corral and pulled her saddle off. Feeling a wave of nausea, I dunked my head in the cool water of the stock tank. My nerves started to settle and I walked back into the cabin. I had a fully stocked doctor's bag in the chuck wagon that had been abandoned at Navasota Crossing after the war by a doctor who would never need it again. I had been an orderly in the hospital at Camp Stephen Douglas while I was a prisoner. The Yankee doctors had let me do a lot, but nothing to prepare me for this.

There was a tin cup and a crock on the table full of cool water. On one of the shelves I spotted some clean dish towels and a couple of bottles of whiskey. I filled the cup with a mixture of half water and whiskey. With the cup at his lips, he opened his pale blue eyes. "Mister, my name is Aaron Turner. I found you outside. I'm gonna do my best to help ya. You're hurt too bad to move and I ain't got anybody to help me, so we'll just make do the best we can."

He nodded weakly, slowly draining the cup. The markings on the arrow were Kiowa. Lord knows I'd seen enough of them in my day. With the greasy, bloody buckskin shirt cut away, I washed off as much of the dirt and blood that I could. I poured whiskey in the wound and on my knife.

I offered my unnamed friend more to drink, but he didn't respond. The arrow had entered next to his right shoulder blade and wedged between two ribs. I made a narrow slit to open the wound wider. I didn't feel the arrowhead.

"I'm sorry. I'm gonna have to go deeper." There was no response, but his breathing was still shallow. I widened and deepened the cut. This time, the knife blade scraped on metal. The edges of the arrowhead were gripped by the bottom of the rib above it and the top of the rib below it.

"Okay, Mister. This is gonna hurt." I wiggled the shaft of the arrow and felt the point move slightly. I managed to get the tip of the knife blade under the edge of the arrowhead. This time as I pulled up on the shaft, I pried upward with the knife. The shaft and arrow slipped free. Bright red blood poured from the wound. There were no bubbles coming up through the blood. If the sac around the lung had been opened, air would be bubbling out. The arrow had not penetrated into the lung; the ribs had stopped it. I blotted up as much blood as I could with the dish towels, poured whiskey down the wound, and applied pressure until the bleeding stopped. Bandages made from strips of old sheets worked well to wrap around his chest.

Rolling him gently onto his back, I placed the pillow under his head and covered him lightly with a quilt. His eyes opened when he was offered another cup of whiskey and water. He drained the cup. "My name's Aaron Turner."

He smiled weakly and a hint of a twinkle flickered across his eyes. "I know. You already told me. My name is Luis bon Chance, all my life I've been just plain Chance. Thank you for what you done."

My mind swirled trying to decide what to do. Pecos could handle the herd without me, if there was even still a herd. Surely they had been able to gather the cattle. I was needed here. But every hour, every day, I stayed here, the less likely I would find the herd at all.

My hands were shaking. A good dose of straight whiskey set me up. I decided to take a look around. The lean-to held a milk cow and a fine Hereford bull. The nesting boxes in the shed held several eggs which I put in my hat. There was a rickety outhouse, a small garden, pecan and fruit trees. There were mustard greens in the garden. I picked a mess and took them inside.

Chance raised up on an elbow, winced and asked for water. He drank two cups of water laced with whiskey. "Thank you, son. I was comin' in from the outhouse about daylight. Five Kiowa were right on me. They stole some horses, but my stallion got away. I don't know if they got my cattle."

"I seen some nice Hereford cross-breds about two miles from here. You think they was yours?"

"Yeah. I imagine that's them. Nobody else has got anything like that around here."

It was past noon. I found some cornmeal, salt, smoked bacon and a can of lard. I washed the greens carefully to get the little bugs and dirt off, brought them to a boil, then poured off the water, rinsed them and started cooking slowly until they were tender, adding a little bacon grease. I fried some bacon and made a pan of passable cornbread.

"Son, that all shore tasted good. They say greens builds up your blood."

He had eaten much more than I expected. There sure weren't any leftovers for the chickens.

A sack of pinto beans was on a shelf. I picked out all the rocks and rinsed them real well, then started soaking them for supper. "Chance, I'm gonna ride around for a look. I need to leave a gun with you. He pointed to a peg on the rear wall. A beautiful pair of well worn

Walker Colt pistols hung in a saddle holster. I laid them across his bed. "Loaded?"

"I didn't git this old by bein' stupid, boy."

The longhorns had made themselves right at home with their new companions on the lush pasture. I circled back and forth until I finally found horse tracks heading northeast. Five unshod horses and several wearing shoes. I tracked them to where I found they had driven the stolen livestock to the banks of the Red River, but I dared not cross. I didn't know what mischief might lie in wait across the muddy water and was in no mood to find out. The Kiowa were probably already halfway back to their reservation telling the Indian agent they had found horses that had strayed into Indian Territory.

I found myself in a difficult situation. I had a responsibility to a dozen men and was responsible for five wagons, a chuck wagon and sixteen hundred head of cattle, twenty mules, and fifty head of cow ponies. But I had stumbled upon a situation where a lonely injured man needed me desperately. Pecos or Matt could handle things for a while without me. Chance would certainly die without me. The decision was made. The consequence would be whether or not I would be able to catch up to the herd. Traveling alone in the Nations was a dangerous proposition. It was a personal decision and risk I must take to be able to live with myself.

When I returned, Chance seemed much better. He was sitting up on the side of the bed. "I made it to the outhouse by myself while you was gone. Took me a while to get there and back, but I made it. Let's celebrate me feelin' better with some more of that whiskey. If we run out of the first bottle, I got another." The whiskey seemed to loosen his tongue and ease his pain.

"Aaron Turner? Red hair, blue eyes, tall. Who are your parents, son?"

"Aaron and Nancy Turner of Navasota Crossing, in Leon County."

"By golly, I thought that you was Aaron and Nancy's boy. I

knowed them all my life since I was sixteen. Fine, fine folks. Are they still livin'?"

"My father died in '51 when I was only a year old. I really didn't know him. Mother is still alive. She lives in Groesbeck next door to my half-brother, Marcus King."

"I remember Marcus well. Your Momma was one of the finest women I ever knew. I came to Texas with your Daddy in 1817. We had a mule train of goods and traded our way from Natchitoches, Louisiana all the way to San Antonio. Over the years, we fought man-eatin' Karankawa, Comanche, Kiowa, Wichita, outlaws, and Mexican soldiers. We fought together at the siege of San Antonio and at San Jacinto and a dozen lesser fights. He was a fierce fighter, but as good, honest and just man as I ever met. You know he was a Methody preacher? He was a big tall man with red hair and blue eyes. Kinda serious fella. He was a major in the Republic militia, promoted to lieutenant colonel. When we went with Winfield Scott to Mexico he got promoted to full colonel."

He drank another cup of whiskey and continued to unburden his soul. One story followed another far into the night. Chance told me his whole life story, and more about my father than I had ever known. I hung on every word.

"We used to come up into this country to hunt buffalo and wild horses. I made a friend, a Wichita warrior called Many Coups. He called me Many Peoples because I spoke so many languages. He had a beautiful wife called Singing Bird."

"During the days of the Republic, the militia got called out to fight the Wichita. I tried to get Many Coups to leave for the Nations, but he wouldn't go, but he did send Singing Bird. He got killed in the battle. I buried him there with full Wichita honors. Thank God I wasn't the one who killed him."

"Not long after the Mexican War, my wife, Amanda, and all three of my children died of cholera. I rode to the Nations and searched until I found Singing Bird and her children. I brought them here. They have all been dead for fifteen years." He wiped tears from his eyes and refilled his cup. The stories he had needed to tell for so long had now been told. He tossed off the cup, wiped his mouth, lay back on the bed and fell asleep.

I made a pallet on the porch as it was cooler. I had learned more about my father in one night than I had ever known. I fell asleep dreaming of the man I longed to know.

———

I awoke to find Chance standing on the porch. "I can git to the outhouse by myself."

"Well go, then. You want me to give you a prize?"

"Already been. Stepped over you sleepin' there like a baby. If I'd been an Injun, you'd be missin' your hair." He wheezed out a laugh.

We had coffee, cornbread, bacon and eggs. He ate well and drank half a pot of coffee. Perhaps he was well enough that I could leave. I fixed a few things around the cabin while he sat in a ladder back chair on the porch enjoying the sunshine. He told me of a crossing on the Red River where I should be able to pass easily, and a trail that would join up with the Western Trail.

At supper, he didn't eat much and seemed tired. He looked fevered to me. When I changed his dressing, there was the unmistakable odor of gangrene. Chance noticed it, too.

"Aaron, you and I both know what that stink means. I appreciate all you've done for me. Get me a pencil and paper from that dresser."

"This here bill of sale is for the livestock. This is the deed for my four sections of land. I've signed it over to you. I want you to have everything I got. There ain't nobody else to give it to."

"Now, Chance, you're liable to be fine by morning."

"Boy, you ain't a very good liar and I ain't no fool. You and I both know the smell of death. It's been a good, long life. Bury me next to Singing Bird by the pecan tree."

I sat at his bedside all night as the fever ravaged his body and mind. He called out to Amanda and his children. He called out for Singing Bird, Many Coups and my father. He barked orders to unseen soldiers.

By dawn his breathing was shallow and the smell of death hung heavy in the room. He opened his eyes, reached out his hands and called, "I'm coming!" He sighed and died with a faint smile on his face.

I cried like a baby. This man I had only known two days had

———— **76** ————

touched my life deeply. He had become a friend and now he was gone. I had learned so much from him in that short time. I would never forget him.

I wrapped him in the quilt and laid him in a grave next to Singing Bird. I placed a board at the head of his grave simply carved, "Chance."

12

Late May, 1877, Northwest Texas Frontier
Reunited

A CAST IRON POT, SKILLET, coffee pot, utensils, cornmeal, beans, bacon, and coffee were piled on the small table. I stuffed them in a clean flour sack. There was a good wool blanket and an old wagon tarp that would do for a bedroll.

As I gathered up things for the trip, I heard a terrible racket coming from the porch where I had left Moon tied and saddled. There was a handsome bay stallion sniffing and nuzzling her and expressing his "interest." Moon was stomping her feet and nipping at the stud horse. It was obvious she was in season. In the blink of an eye he had accomplished his purpose, walked into the corral and drank from the water tank. He wore a look of proud accomplishment, but also a halter and broken lead rope. The Kiowa raiders had not gotten away with him. Chance had told me the horse was called Houston in honor of Sam Houston.

I noticed he was wearing shoes. You only put shoes on a horse you intended to ride, so I assumed he was broke. Moon's saddle fit him pretty well. I tied my long rawhide rope to his halter and walked, trotted, then loped him in circles in the corral. He responded like a champion. I found a headstall with a Tom Thumb bit I assumed was his. It fit perfectly. He accepted it like a gentleman. I stepped into the left stirrup. He stood quietly. I repeated the process a few times without difficulty. I finally swung a leg over and found the right stirrup. He never made a step.

With the easiest touch of spurs, he eased into a walk. I gradually took him through his paces. This was a well trained stallion. He had an easy trot and a smooth lope. He could turn on a dime, and backed up like a gold-plated charm.

I opened the gate and rode him down to the cattle. He knew exactly what to do. He was almost as good as Moon. I put the saddle back on her, and fitted him with panniers. I gathered the last of my things and was just about ready to hit the road.

Bacon, eggs, cornbread and a whole pot of coffee got me ready for the day ahead. Extra bacon and cornbread were wrapped in a rag and placed in the saddlebags. I was ready to leave riding Moon and leading the stud, who was serving as a lowly packhorse today.

I scouted ahead without the cattle to make sure I had the right place. The crossing on the Red River was not hard to find. The bottom was firm and the sides not too steep. I could see where a mixed group of shod and unshod horses had crossed since the last rain. I could only assume the tracks were left by the Kiowa raiding party. There was a faint trail angling northwest that joined the Western Trail in five or six miles.

I rode back and started the small herd toward the crossing. Thanks to the previously irritating longhorns that were quite used to river crossings, the cattle stepped into the muddy red water like they had been doing it all their lives. I let them graze briefly north of the river before moving them along. One man couldn't afford to push them too hard, but just nudge them in the general direction and keep them moving slowly. By late afternoon, we were on the Western Trail. There was good grass, fresh water and a good camp site; it was time to call it a day. There was a recently used campsite with a pile of rocks shaped like an arrow pointing north. There was the corner of a red bandana sticking out. Under the bandana was a note written in Pecos' less than grammatical hand.

"Aron, hop ur ok. We finly got them strays gathered an on the trail. They is a hakberry tree behin you with a sac of jerky, salt an a lil cofe. Ketch up kwick as u kin."

Pecos

My spirits soared as I realized that the herd and my friends weren't very far away. To be honest, I was feeling pretty low. If Pecos could write as well he could cowboy, he would be a new Shakespeare. Obviously, that wasn't going to happen.

I set up camp and unsaddled Moon and pulled the panniers off Sam Houston. I lead them to a pretty little stream. I'll be darn if Moon didn't give Sam the 'come here big boy' snicker that he instantly understood. With a little foot stomping and nipping, the stud bred her again. This was one of those things I just didn't have time to be tending to right now.

"Moon, you're worse than some of those dance hall girls in Dodge City! You oughta be ashamed of yourself."

Bacon and cornbread washed down with a whole pot of coffee got me settled in for the night. The quail were calling and the fireflies twinkling. My life so far had prepared me to be where I was. I stretched out to sleep with my guns at my side.

After a quick breakfast and some extra grub for eating in the saddle, I led the horses to the creek to drink. Sam decided to try his luck with Moon. She bit him on the neck, gave him both back feet in the chest and an angry threatening squeal. "You tell 'em, Moon! Guess you're out of luck, Sam."

I rode the dejected stallion that day and let Moon carry the pack saddles. The country here was rolling with low hills, small valleys and streams. Red oaks, hackberry, elm, locust and cedars punctuated the landscape. There were huge old cottonwood trees along the creeks. I saw deer, turkey, cottontails and squirrels. A curious coyote followed my little herd for a while. Finally, I dropped Moon's lead rope, set the spurs to Sam, and galloped down full speed at the surprised predator. He was heading south toward Texas with his tail-bushed out like a haystack as fast as he could go. It was the first time I'd laughed in a long time.

Parts of the trail started to look familiar from my one previous trip. Twelve miles north there was a good campsite. It was about as far as one man could move cattle by himself in a day. I hobbled the horses and let them graze as I stirred up some supper. The stock enjoyed the lush native grasses. It was obvious another larger herd had been through only a couple of days before; the cow pies were just starting to dry.

After another good day and a night on the trail heading north, I put away the breakfast dishes, saddled up and eased the cattle onto the trail. Before mid-morning, I thought I could see a wisp of dust to the north. I eased the Winchester out of the rifle boot and laid it across my lap. I headed the horses into the trees until I could identify the source of the dust.

A lone rider on a blue roan horse was heading south at a long trot. I knew that profile and that horse. It was Levi Carter! I eased the horses where they could be seen and waved my hat. When he recognized me, he kicked his horse into a lope. I galloped to meet him.

"Aaron! We thought you'd run for Jericho! How you been?"

I gave him the short version of my unforgettable journey. There were parts I couldn't tell anyone, not even Pecos.

"The herd's only about five miles ahead. It come a big rain, the North Fork of the Red is out of its banks. We set up waitin' for it to go down. I'll help you move these cows. We ought to be there for dinner."

"Well, I had to spend the night out on the prairie by myself. I made a fire to dry out my clothes and cook some of the meat I had butchered off the dead steers. I come up on this little homestead the next day. There was an old man with an arrow in his back. I thought he was dead, but he was still barely alive. I cut the arrow out of him. He came around pretty good that night. We talked some. Come to find out he was a good friend of my Daddy, from way back to 1817. He told me a lot of stories I sure was glad to hear. Poor ol' man got gangrene and died. He deeded me four sections of range land in Wilbarger County, these cattle, a bull and this stud horse." They asked lots more questions. I answered most of 'em, and evaded the others. There were some things that I just couldn't talk about. That short span of time had deeply affected me.

It took three days for the river to drop enough to swim the cattle across. We returned to Comanche Springs on Big Elk Creek. Kelly fed us well, as always. The wagons were forted up like usual in Cheyenne territory. I leaned back against a wagon wheel and listened as Jake and Matt played their fiddle and guitar. They had been teaching Kirby how to play and he was making steady progress. I lit my pipe and smoked a couple of bowls of tobacco while I listened. Camp settled into the nightly pattern of riders coming on and off shift. Sleep escaped me again. The memories of this place brought back memories of my sense of guilt along with the ghosts of white men and Indians that walked the night.

Another day's travel brought us to Soldier Springs. Most everybody swam and cleaned up in the clear water. The huge lonely cottonwood tree and the tumbling waterfall had made this one of our favorite places. I was glad to join in with the others.

The trail north to the Washita was marked with lush grass and sunny skies. However, Fort Supply was almost a ghost town. The soldiers had been reassigned to duty elsewhere and most of the town's inhabitants had left with them. Even the saloon had closed.

After supper, Kelly and I sat on the bank of the Washita hoping to catch some catfish. "I was pretty scared alone on the prairie. I was worse scared when I started diggin' the arrow outta the ol' man. I was scared he might die. When he did, I cried like a baby." I relit my pipe and Kelly adjusted his chewing tobacco.

"He told you things you never knowed about your Daddy. You found a link to your past and a friend, then lost 'em in two days. Reckon it would be hard on anybody. You woulda liked my Daddy, Aaron. His name was Billy Ray Webb. He was as good a man as God made. He loved to read the Bible, and even preached sometimes. That man loved to sing good ol' country gospel. He liked huntin' and fishin' and was always real good to my Momma and us kids."

The fish weren't hungry. Neither one of us ever even got a bite. Neither one cared.

———

Side oats and blue grama grasses were knee deep on the horses. The buffalo was thick, curly and green in between the taller plants. The days were warm, but not too hot. The nights cooled off enough to be comfortable. Luke and Levi kept us supplied with fresh deer meat. The river crossings were easy and the cattle gained weight as they ambled up the trail. Three nights in a row there was almost no moon. After midnight each night, there was an almost magical display of falling stars in the northeastern sky. Bright white stars, mingled with reddish, green and bright yellow falling stars. Some would cross the whole sky from horizon to horizon; others were gone in a flash. It was one of the most remarkable things we ever saw and talked about again many times.

Four days after crossing the Cimarron, the cottonwoods along the Arkansas were finally in view. Dodge City just across the river. The cattle buyer for Joseph McCoy rode out and visited a while. He remarked these were the best cattle we had ever brought to market. We shook hands on thirty dollars a head, then set up camp on the banks of the river. I had first crossed this mighty river a lifetime ago and hundreds of miles away at Arkansas Post under the big guns of Fort Hindman as a twelve year old courier in the Confederate Army in 1862.

13

August 3, 1877, Dodge City, Kansas
One door opens, another closes

WE SWAM THE CATTLE across the Arkansas and delivered them to the shipping pens. The wagons crossed by the bridge. We followed our time honored tradition of banking, bathing and feasting. The Dodge City bank was now a fully completed brick structure. I could remember banking at Caldwell, Kansas in a tent with a big safe and four armed guards. I liked this better.

I guess one Chinese bath house and laundry was about the same as another. We all knew the routine now. The close shave with a straight razor felt good to cut off my wiry copper-colored whiskers. My hair had gotten long, shaggy and greasy. Even if a fellow tried, there was just so much you could do washing up on the side of some creek in Indian Territory. They did their best to wash, starch and iron my trail clothes, but I had worn them plumb out and would throw them away as soon as I bought some more. I noticed that Zach and Tyler actually needed a shave, while with Kirby and Keenan it was largely symbolic.

Kelly had cleaned up pretty good. He was in charge of the "young herd" while we were in town. The older ones did their shopping north of the tracks, but then I saw Pecos, Matt, Jake, Kyle, Levi and Luke checking in their guns to visit south of the line. I was used to seeing Pecos and Matt heading that direction, but I wasn't quite ready to see the others head that direction. They weren't boys any more. They were grown men.

I sold the buffalo hides to the same buyer. "Well, Texas, ain't ya gonna watch me count 'em this year?"

"I counted 'em good when I bought 'em. I don't think the rats ate any. There weren't many hides to be bought at Fort Griffin. Looks like things are playin' out. 'Bout the same up here?"

"The only hides I get come from Texas and they tell me it's all done down there. I've already started buyin' buffalo bones. You know they use them for everythin' from fertilizer to makin' fine china? They don't bring much. I guess if a fella was comin' with empty wagons they would pay for his trip, but there's not much money to be made. A man might see a little herd of buffalo here and there, but they're pretty much gone."

———————

I found my way back to the Liquor and Tobacco Store to stock back up on their house blend number seven. I had become pretty fond of it and enjoyed it almost every day. The fragrant smoke curling around my head relaxed me. The sealed metal tins kept it good indefinitely.

"Light as air, strong as whiskey, cheap as dirt! Come have a look at what will forever change the face of cattle country!" I had to see this. A salesman had built a corral in the alley behind the store out of stout cedar posts and twisted wire. The wire had sharp barbs sticking out about every four inches. Inside the corral were half a dozen snuffy longhorn steers. They challenged the tight wire repeatedly, but the sharp barbs turned them back with bloody hides and noses.

"Set a solid post every sixteen to twenty feet, stretch out and staple up five or more strands of wire, and you've got yourself a fence. Got good cattle? Keep your neighbor's scruffy bull out. Got an expensive bull? Keep him in. Keeps your stock from strayin'. You'll need fewer hands to gather 'em."

"How much does this cost?"

"Sir, with your posts and labor, it will cost you a hundred and fifty dollars to build a whole mile for the wire and staples for a five wire fence."

I walked off down the alley thinking about fencing the ranch. I looked up and was shocked by what I saw. There was a twenty foot tall wooden tower topped with a metal fan and a tail lettered ECLIPSE. As the fan turned, a gear box raised and lowered wooden rods which disappeared into a metal pipe. Part of the way down the metal pipe was a T-joint from which another metal pipe discharged a steady stream of clean, clear water into a metal tank.

"The ECLIPSE windmill with an eight foot metal fan can pump three thousand gallons of water a day, every day the wind blows. If you want a twelve or sixteen foot fan, it'll pump even more."

"What's that?" I asked in amazement.

"That is the most modern invention for diggin' water wells in the world, sir. It's a walkin' beam cable tool drillin' rig. Let me try to explain. The mule walks in a circle to turn that big gear on top of that post. Because it's so strong, we call it a Sampson post. That gear operates this special gear called a Pittman gear. It's just like what you see on the drive wheels of a train engine. It changes a rotary motion to a side-to-side motion. That long rod connects it to the walkin' beam by a T-gear. Every time the Pittman rod goes back and forth, the walkin' beam goes up and down. The far end of the walkin' beam is attached to a heavy oiled rope that runs through a gear at the top of the cable rig tool tower. It lets the bit fall into the hole and raises it back up. Every time it falls, it drives a little deeper into the ground. It'll go through about anything from sand to solid rock; the harder the ground the slower the drillin'. Every so often, you got to pour a little water in the hole, you swing the bailer over the hole. It brings up dirt, mud, sand, rock chips, whatever has accumulated at the bottom of the hole. How deep is the water on your place, sir?"

"We hand dug a well and hit good water at thirty feet. Took three of us, working every day, nine days."

"This rig would drill it all in one day unless there's a lot of rock, then it'll take longer. Course the next day you would need to set up the windmill and rod. So in two or three days, two men and a mule could drill the well and set up the windmill."

I was mesmerized by the hypnotic rise and fall of the walking beam. I sat down on a barrel just to watch and think. Pecos and Matt came wandering up smelling of whiskey, but walking straight. "Let me show y'all this new stuff." They looked and wondered at the barbwire, the windmill and the drilling rig.

"Boss, those things could sure change the way we do stuff on the ranch. Dependable water sources will open up huge parts of the range that hardly get used. Fences would make our breedin' program move along faster, and gatherin' cattle wouldn't take no time."

———————

As I walked along Front Street, I was trying to decide what to buy for Momma, Ella, and a little something for Alice. I stopped in one of the larger mercantile stores and found a dress I knew Mother would like. I got a bag of hard candy for Alice. The clerk said he hadn't ever heard anyone ask if they made it in pickle flavor. A glass display case caught my eye. "Mister, would you pull out that tray of rings, please?" There was a wooden model of a ladies hand for sizing rings. I picked through the rings until I found a pretty gold band just the right size for Ella.

"Somebody is gonna be mighty happy. That ring is fourteen carat gold."

"I hope she's pretty happy with the cowboy that comes with the ring." I continued to wander around in the store. "Mister, do y'all carry plans for buildin' a house that list everything you need to build it?"

"Sure, do, Tex. Let me show ya the Sears and Roebuck catalogue. They got everything from mansions to outhouses."

I spent some time thumbing through the catalogue until I saw just what I wanted. It had two bedrooms, a big kitchen and dining room with a big den. There were porches on the front and back with an indoor bathroom, complete with a big copper bathtub. I upgraded to the best cook stove and oven, with an extra large hot water reservoir in the side. There was a nice pot-belly stove for the den. There were two outside doors with glass windows and doorknobs, and screen doors. There were also glass windows carefully crated to avoid breakage, plus a hundred little things I never would have thought to buy. When it was tallied up, paid out, and loaded, it filled two wagons.

———————

Kyle, Jake, Luke and Levi had come weaving back into camp pretty well pickled a couple of hours after dark. They were loud and singing. The younger ones sure got their eyes full. Finally, well past midnight, Pecos and Matt came galloping their horses across the bridge.

"You boys run outta money?"

Pecos grinned. "Nah, Aaron. It was more like we run outta friends. I won a big hand in a poker game and some of them buffalo hunters got kinda upset. That bartender's shotgun calmed 'em down long enough for us to git to our horses."

"How much did ya win?"

"Over five hundred dollars, a gold watch and a pair of false teeth." Pecos got a laughing fit and Matt had to slap him on the back. "I throwed him back his teeth."

———————

There were some subdued cowboys around the breakfast fire that morning. Sometimes a little bit of fun goes a long way. I took Keenan, Kirby, Tyler and Zach back into Dodge with me in the two empty freight wagons and the chuck wagon. I bought a walking beam cable tool rig with all the bits and bailers and cables, plus an eight foot ECLIPSE windmill with all the necessary pipe. Where ever we could find the room, we stacked on rolls of barbed wire, and on top of all of this, our groceries.

Once again we headed our wagons and horse herd home to Texas. The Cimarron was behind us, as gentle as a kitten this year. The store at Fort Supply was open for business to passing herds and a few local folks. They didn't buy much. The town had died when the fort closed. We pushed further south finally coming to Soldier Springs. Our next stop was the most beautiful on the trail, Comanche Springs. The beautiful grassland stretched away to the west. The red sandstone bluffs stood sentinel above the crystal clear waters of Big Elk Creek and the two graves along its western bank. When we reached the North Fork of the Red River, I took Matt with me and split off cross-country back to the shack in Wilbarger County.

I retrieved the pair of Walker Colts, and led the Hereford bull, milk cow and her heifer calf behind the horses. We left the chickens and hogs to fend for themselves. We spent the night on the trail and rode into Vernon the next morning.

As I was registering the deed in the Wilbarger County Clerk's office, there was a man doing business just down the counter. "Excuse me for eaves droppin'. I heard you are registerin' the deed from Luis bon Chance's four sections. It joins my land, and I've tried to buy it for years, but he didn't want to sell it. I'd sure like to make you an offer on it. Don Robinson is my name."

"Turner. Aaron Turner. What are you offerin'?"

"The going price on unimproved range land around here is a dollar an acre if it's been surveyed. I know his has. That would be two thousand five hundred and sixty."

"Give me a few minutes, Mr. Robinson. I'll be back."

We walked across the street to the barber shop. "I want a shave."

"You ain't from around here."

"No, I ain't. Does that affect the price of the shave?" I laughed.

"No, I reckon not."

While he lathered my face and started to shave, I started to ask a few question. "I buried an ol' friend of my daddy up near the Red River. Older man, probably near eighty. Everybody called him Chance."

The men playing checkers stopped, and the barber shop became real quite. "Why, Mister, we all knowed Ol' Chance. He was kinda an ol' hoot owl stayin' out there all by hisself. We all liked him. He's dead?"

"I guess so. I ain't gonna take the trouble to bury a man that ain't dead. He had got an arrow from the Kiowa. I cut it out, but he got gangrene and died. Turns out he and my daddy was friends goin' way back."

"What's your name, son?"

"My name's Aaron Turner."

"Ol' Chance, I heard him talk about a man named Aaron Turner. Chance scouted for him in the Texas Revolution and the Mexican War. Seemed to talk real highly of him."

"I know the ol' man was good as gold. He deeded me his stock and land. I got a fellow wantin' to buy the land name of Don Robinson.

Claims he was Chance's neighbor. Can you think of any reason ol' Chance wouldn't want his land sold to him?"

"We all know him. He seems honest and works hard. His ranch joins Chance's place. Now it don't bother me a bit, but seems like Don's part Wichita Indian." I paid for the shave and free information.

I returned to the Clerk's office. "Mr. Turner, while you been thinkin', I'm going to bump my offer to three thousand dollars even."

"Done." The paperwork was transferred and Matt and I soon rejoined Pecos and the crew at Doan's Store. "Drinks are on me. My friend Chance is buyin' one last round."

———————

We pushed on to Fort Griffin and delivered the goods to Mrs. Nixon and Cooper. Kirby and Keenan were glad to see their mother, but I was kind of sorry to see the little rats go.

We made it on down to Belle Plain without any trouble. Kelly stood up on the wagon seat. "Would you look at that?"

The town and the college had literally risen out of the ground in quarried limestone walls and tile roofs. It was a really pretty little place. The college was as big as any building I had seen anywhere in Texas except the capitol. In the center of town, the footings for a courthouse were laid out.

"Hello, Captain Tyus! Looks like a whole Corps of Yankee Engineers has been at work. What's gonna happen if Belle Plain don't become the county seat?"

"Then I will be living in a very large house!" He laughed.

14

November 5, 1877, Turner Ranch, Callahan County, Texas
Changes

"MEASURE IT AGAIN, TYLER. That don't look right."

"Well, I ain't never claimed to be no kinda carpenter."

"We been tryin' to figure these measurements and stakes and strings all mornin'. Can we be that stupid?"

Kelly's unmistakable voice boomed out behind us. "Howdy, boys. Looks like you need some help. Little Jake, get my tool box down for me."

"I didn't know you was a carpenter?"

"I ain't, Aaron. But I've had my hand in buildin' and rebuildin' lots of barns, sheds, chicken houses, and corn cribs. But I brought tools and a big basket of food. Reckon that'll help?"

While we ate, Little Jake started a small fire for coffee. Kelly went over the plans, pulled out a carpenter's measuring tape and started checking measurements. "A lot of folks will get the sides the right length, but the house ain't square. That's why we gotta do these measurements from corner to corner." By the time we had finished our lunch and a cup of coffee, Kelly had it laid out and cross-checked.

We grabbed shovels and picks and started digging out the foundation footing. By dark, all the footings had been dug, back-filled with rocks, gravel and cement. The footings went twelve inches deep and wooden forms raised them above ground level twenty four inches. A big level kept us honest.

"Let that dry two days and we'll come back and help ya start buildin'."

"Thanks for the food and help, Biscuit and Little Jake."

———

Pecos wiped his face on a sweat stained sleeve. "Just why are we buildin' a house anyway when we got a good tight dugout? I'll betcha a dollar this has somethin' to do with Ella Fisher back in Groesbeck."

I felt my face turning red. "Yeah, maybe."

"We're breakin' our backs on a 'Maybe?' Have you even asked her?"

"Not exactly."

"We're usin' picks and shovels on 'Not exactly'?" Pecos was enjoying my discomfort.

"Well I bought her a gold ring in Dodge City, and I'm gonna ask her when we get back to Limestone County."

"And what if she says 'Ain't no way she's marryin' your ugly face?'"

"Then I'll be livin' in a nice big house while you live in that ol' dugout!"

———

"Boss, I can ride anything with four legs, rope any cow on the place, turn cows in a stampede, cross flooded rivers, and take a herd from Texas all the way to Kansas, but this house buildin' is complicated!" Pecos had a point.

From the floor, to the walls, to the rafters, the house gradually took shape in the pecan grove above the flood plain of Pecan Bayou. Once the sheet metal was up on the roof, it started to look like a house. Kelly framed in the windows and doors.

It took all five of us to move the pot-belly and cook stoves into place. "If we don't follow the instructions to the letter for puttin' in the stovepipe, the whole durn house could burn down around your ears. It ain't any of your business how I know. I best do this part myself." Kelly groused.

Both stoves worked well and the pipes didn't leak smoke. There was metal flashing to protect the wood and seal the holes in the walls, ceiling and roof. Careful checking showed the wooden frame wasn't getting hot anywhere near the pipe. While Kelly had been busy installing the stovepipes, we had been building the box and strip outside and interior walls. All the detail work with cabinets, drawers, knobs and latches seemed to take forever, but still something seemed unfinished. "I forgot to buy any paint!"

"You're gonna spoil that gal puttin' her in a painted house. She'll have you doin' all the chores." Pecos seemed to think this was funny.

I broke out about an acre of good level ground close to the house for a garden and fenced it with new barbed wire. Tyler got tangled up in it, tore his shirt and cut his arm. "I betcha hell is plumb full of this stuff!" We laughed at him but felt the same way.

We built a barn and tack room, chicken house and outhouse. We fenced a trap of about twenty acres from the barn down to the creek for the milk cow and horses. Tyler leaned against a post. "It looks good. I'm glad it's finally done."

"We're not near done until we get a well dug and a windmill up. We're just gettin' started good."

We set up the Sampson post, manhandled the big gears into place, and installed the giant see-saw beam six feet up in the air. We built a windmill tower about twenty feet tall from hardwoods cut along the creek and braced with oak lumber. We hung the stout hoist just below the top of the tower and ran a heavily oiled one inch manila rope from the walking beam through the hoist.

I fumbled repeatedly trying to weave the end of the rope back into itself to secure it to the drill bit. "Good grief, I can drive a herd of cattle from Texas all the way to Kansas, but I can't figure out this stinkin' knot!"

"Care if I try, Aaron?" We had borrowed Zach Barton for some extra help. He sat down with the diagram. After a couple of false starts, he got the complex knot exactly right. "There you go, Boss." He just grinned as we looked on in amazement.

We attached the T-bar to the opposite end of the walking beam and fastened it to the Pitman rod. We spun the cedar pole that turned the heavy gears. The Pitman rod moved back, then forward. The T-bar pivoted, raised and lowered the beam, causing the rope to raise and lower the drill bit.

We harnessed a mule to the end of the cedar pole and began to walk him in circles. He stumbled on the Pitman rod the first few times, but soon knew exactly where it lay and stepped over it after that.

As the spudder bit rose and fell, it slowly punched a hole deeper and deeper into the ground. We poured a little water into the forming hole to soften it up. After a hole had been made about three feet deep, we switched to the heavy bailer. It dropped straight down into the hole and brought up the loose dirt and rock which we discharged to the side.

The process continued monotonously until at about twenty-five feet we could feel and hear the bit striking rock. Each drop of the bit hardly advanced the cable at all. Tyler poured a little more water down the hole. The mule continued to walk in an endless circle, leaving a bare path and mule droppings. The clanging continued as the pointed end of the spudder struck the rocky layer.

Finally, there was a subtle change in the sound of the bit and the vibration of the rope. The bit started to advance as much as an inch per stroke. We stopped and bailed out the sharp rock chips.

Pecos ran the rocks through his fingers. "There's a little gravel mixed in with the rock chips. We may be about to get somewhere."

This time, we didn't add any water to the hole. The bit advanced several inches with each stroke. It didn't take long to advance the cable three feet.

"Bail it out, boys."

The bailer clattered down the hole, hitting the bottom with a distinct crunching sound. When we turned it over to dump the contents, it was filled with damp gravel and muddy water.

Around and around the mule turned the cedar pole. The walking beam relentlessly went up and down. The cable turned in the hoist as the spudder bit rose and fell. Each time the bailer was emptied, there was more water. Finally, at about forty feet, we hit solid rock again. Several strikes made no more progress.

"We got ourselves a well!"

We removed the bit and began to lower ten foot joints of three inch pipe into the hole. Each joint was threaded so the ends would screw together with our hands first, then with large pipe wrenches. There was finally enough pipe threaded together to reach the bottom of the hole to keep it from caving in. We screwed on a final joint of pipe and topped it with a T shaped fitting where we attached our discharge pipe.

We cooked our supper outside on the ground, but we moved our bedrolls inside the newly built house. I sat with my friends on the back porch smoking my pipe. We were all so tired, no one had to rock us to sleep. It felt strange to be sleeping on a wooden floor under a real roof.

Zach, Tyler and Pecos rolled out to eat some of my cooking. It was just bacon and cornbread, with a big pot of Arbuckle's coffee. It wasn't fancy, but it would get us through the day.

The pumping mechanism was a simple wooden ball inside a brass cage that allowed water to enter, but not leave. This was screwed onto the end of a ten foot wooden rod. This was attached to a series of rods all the way to the top of the tower. The rods had oiled leather cups that folded away as the rods went down into the well and opened as the rods were raised, pulling a column of water to the discharge pipe.

Zach pulled the wagon as close as he could to the tower. "Easy, boy. We don't wanna knock 'er down!" The gear box of the windmill was tied on to the hoist and hitched to the mule.

"Easy does it, Tyler." He led the mule slowly forward. As the gear box began to rise, Zach pulled on a side rope to keep it from banging into the tower, while Pecos and I scrambled up the tower to keep it from getting caught under the cross bars. When it finally got as high as we could lift it with the hoist, we tied it off to keep it from falling. All four of us were precariously balanced on the small platform that topped the tower. By brute force, we lifted the gear box through the hole and bolted it in place.

The fan was easier. It was made in sections, which the mule

hoisted up and we dragged around the sides of the platform. They were the newer metal type which were much lighter than the older wooden fans. The sections bolted together and the whole fan attached to the gear.

The great wind vane came next with ECLIPSE painted on both sides. It was a little tricky to attach, as it had to be able to fold away when the well was not in use. A flat iron ran down to a lever on the lower tower to engage the wind vane.

"Tyler, pull the lever and lock 'er down."

As he engaged the tail, the wind caught it and swung the fan directly into the face of the wind. The fan immediately began to turn and the wooden rods began to rise and fall. As the column of water began to fill within the pipe, the rods moved less easily. The fan continued to turn and work the rods. Soon a trickle of muddy water spilled from the discharge pipe.

"Is that it?" Zach looked pretty disappointed.

With each succeeding stroke of the rods, the stream of water became stronger until at last a full flow of slightly dirty water poured from the pipe. I ran to catch a handful.

"It's good sweet water. As soon as the dirt settles, we're going to have all we can use."

Everyone else crowded around to get a taste, then let the water pour over their heads. It didn't take long for Zach and Tyler to be standing under the full flow of the cool water.

Within two days, the water was as clear and clean as anyone could have wanted. I shut down the well, locked back the tail and started packing. It was time for a trip back to see Ella in Limestone County.

———

"Mrs. Fisher, that sure was a fine supper."

"You're just tryin' to get on my good side." she grinned.

"Hell, Elizabeth, he ate like a starvin' wolf, just like when that coyote got in your chickens last year." Mr. Fisher sat picking his teeth and trying to look mean. "We shot that rascal!"

"Daddy, you be nice!"

"It's kinda nice outside, not too cold. Would you like to go for a walk, Ella?"

"Yes, I would. It's kinda smelly over here by Daddy." Mr. Fisher just sat with a guilty grin on his face.

We were hardly past the yard gate when I reached in my pocket for a small box. I fingered it carefully, pulled it out and opened it. "Uhm, Ella? Would you, ah..."

"The answer is yes, Aaron Turner." She gave me a great big kiss and pulled me back to the house. "Momma, look what I found!"

"Why that's a real gold ring. I wonder who could have lost it? Does it fit?"

Ella struggled briefly with the ring. "Yes. It fits just right."

"George, look at the ring Ella found."

"By golly, that's nice! Why didn't you get her somethin' like that, Aaron?"

By this point, I was four shades of purple and red. "Oh heck! I gave it to her. I'm tryin' to ask her to marry me."

"Well, did ya?"

"Did I what?"

"Ask Ella to marry you?"

"I was tryin' to."

"What do ya think, Ella?"

"Well, he's too tall. He's got red curly hair and blue eyes, but I guess he's the best I can do."

Mrs. Fisher scratched her head. "Don't ya think next fall when he gets back from takin' the herd to Dodge would be about right for the wedding?"

"Yes, that would be perfect."

All three of them burst out laughing, hugging and patting me on the back. It had to have been one of the worst marriage proposals in the history of Texas. But just the same, I was going to marry Ella!

———————

I rode to the Belle Plain court house and filed on four sections directly south of the house for fifty cents an acre and fifty cents for surveying. The new tract stretched two miles south and two miles wide. This added thirty two hundred deeded acres to the nineteen hundred we already owned. There was just a little over five thousand acres with live water, and soon it would have windmills and a perimeter fence. My dream was growing.

I had brought plenty of paint back from Groesbeck. It didn't take long for us to have the little house looking like a palace.

We gathered the crew and rode east to the Colorado. We made a wide thorough sweep looking for any mavericks that had been missed in previous drives. To our surprise, we drove over four hundred head of mostly straight longhorns back to the ranch. It took a few days to get them all worked. There were at least two hundred and fifty that would be ready for the market, not counting our home-raised cross bred cattle.

We spent two weeks cutting and peeling cedar posts. We saved those larger than eight inches in diameter for corner and gate posts. We started building fence north of the house on the edge of the Callahan Divide. We set the corner post forty-two inches deep, and added heavy brace posts eight feet out west and south. A solid four inch post was cut to fit exactly between the brace and corner posts and wedged into position. We twisted double strands of barbed wire to hold everything tight.

We dug holes and set four or five inch posts every rod, or sixteen and a half feet, all along the eastern property line until we reached the house. Here we set fourteen foot tall eight inch posts four feet deep, ten feet apart. We set a wooden cross bar over the top with my brand burned into it.

We built on down past the house to the creek and set heavy braces back from the creek on both sides. We drove the wagon into the shallow creek bed and stretched the wire across the creek above our heads. Below that, we twisted a double strand of barbed wire. We attached empty wooden barrels continuously across the creek to build a water gap. It was designed so that the barrels would rise and lower with the water level. We continued south along the east property line along the road until we reached the southeast corner post.

Once all the posts were in place we started unrolling the wire. Two of us would carry a roll of wire on a length of pipe between us. When we reached the brace posts we used a horse or mule to drag all the slack we could get out of the wire. Then we would use a wire stretcher to get the last little bit of tightening. Once a wire was in place, Zach and Tyler came behind us nailing staples around the wire into the cedar posts. We had given them sticks marked off with the proper height to keep the strands of wire even. While they nailed, Pecos and I unrolled more wire and stretched it in place. It was a slow process and took all day to hang and staple a quarter mile of fence after the posts had been set.

———————

We had five hundred and eight home raised steers and barren cows, plus the two hundred and fifty longhorns. Our friends at Belle Plain, which was now the growing county seat of Callahan County, had eight hundred and seventy-seven head.

"Cap, that puts us at one thousand six hundred and thirty-five head, our biggest herd yet. Prices are solid, too. I'm buying buffalo bones at Fort Griffin to haul with my freight wagons and planning to back haul trade goods. I'm gonna hire a couple of your college boys to drive the empty wagons as far as Fort Griffin."

15

June 5, 1878, Belle Plain, Callahan County, Texas
North again

IN EARLY MAY, 1878, MOON was big as a barn with her pregnancy. She paced restlessly back and forth in the big corral at the dugout. Her foal had dropped, giving a distinctive pear shape to her belly. The baby was getting in position to come soon. She walked with her tail stuck out behind her like a horse about to drop a load of fertilizer. She stopped to pee every fifteen minutes. Her teats were swollen and dripping milk with every step.

"It won't be long now, girl."

I left her alone in the pen, but I could discretely watch through gaps in the timbers. An hour after full dark she lay down and kicked at her belly. Her legs went straight out, then relaxed when the pain passed. She got up and began to pace again. After the third try, a bulging white sac of fluid appeared. She lay down and began to push and groan. Front feet showed inside the sac, followed by a nose, then a pretty little head. The bag burst open and the foal appeared. Moon stood up and the little horse gently plopped out onto the ground.

Moon used her mouth to remove the remnants of the bag from the baby's nose and mouth. She nuzzled and licked the little body all over. I could see it was a stud colt. His eyes were open and bright and he was breathing well. His coat was solid bay with a small white snip on his nose.

He struggled to sit up, but in just a few minutes he tried to stand. With legs sprawling out in all directions, he fell ungracefully at his mother's feet. On his next attempt, he actually got his feet under him with a little steadying from Moon's nose. She gently guided his muzzle along her belly until he discovered the source of all joy: mother's milk! The slurping was so loud I had to laugh. Once he was full, he unceremoniously flopped down in the straw. Moon had passed the afterbirth and calmly ate it all, while watching her new baby.

I couldn't resist it any longer. "Moon, ol' girl, will ya let me slip in there and see that pretty boy?" She nickered a reply. I knelt by the colt and placed my hand on his neck. He shot upright like a spring and promptly fell over. I stroked his neck, head, legs and belly. Moon nudged me and nibbled on the brim of my hat. I bent down and held his velvet nose in my hand and directed my breath to his nostrils. He would never forget my scent. I named him Uncle Joe in honor of General Joseph Johnston. The colt and I were destined to be friends for the rest of his life.

The wagons rumbled out of Belle Plain toward Clyde with Little Jake and the remuda close behind. The sixteen hundred cattle stood and stretched, falling in behind the horses.

Kelly Ray Webb was as timeless as the plains, never changing. Hardly anything got him rattled. He was a man you could depend on to have hot coffee ready under any circumstances. In his own uneducated fashion, he was a wise man. Wise in the wisdom of men, of people, the way folks thought. He was also my friend. His boy, Little Jake, was a big for his age eleven year old, who knew his job as wrangler and cook's helper, and was learning the tricks to become a working cowboy.

Matt and Jake Dawson were tall, strong slender young men. Matt's work as a blacksmith had given him bulging arm muscles. He could even beat Pecos at arm wrestling. Jake had a smile all the time as wide as the Arkansas River. He never met a stranger, loved to talk and spin tall tales.

Kyle Shepard was tall, blue-eyed, blond and shy. But he wasn't too shy to have a special sweetheart. Cheyenne Boedeker, the prettiest student at Belle Plain College, had set her bonnet for Kyle. He was always easy to get along with and didn't take himself too seriously, but could always be counted on to do his job.

Zach Barton had started out as a lowly wrangler and cook's helper. But his skills had improved until he had become a good cowhand, and would still cook in a pinch. He was skinny, but tough as rawhide. Although he had a dry sense of humor, he took everything pretty serious.

Tyler Beasley was our stray. He had come to us as an orphan off the rowdy dirt streets of Fort Griffin with his brother, Tanner. Tanner lay in a shallow grave at Comanche Springs on Big Elk Creek. Tyler had no family anywhere, so Pecos and I had inherited him as our ranch hand. He worked hard for us and seemed to appreciate everything he got.

Inching north at ten miles a day, the herd raised a cloud of choking dust. The cowboys at drag were taking it pretty hard, so the hands took turns relieving them, except Pecos, Matt and me. Once we were past Fort Griffin, the herd would be able to spread out across the grass and not be confined to the road.

Kirby and Keenan Nixon were watching and waiting for us on the road. We rode together into Fort Griffin and picked up their gear. Robin was by herself. Her sister, Tamara, and niece, Tory, had moved back to east Texas.

Kirby, the sober as a judge, serious as a preacher, older brother, had grown six inches over the winter along with at least a hundred new freckles. Keenan had grown three or four inches himself. He wasn't going to let Kirby get too far ahead of him. And, as much as his brother was serious, Keenan was the exact opposite. He saw the humor in everything and kept us either chasing him down or laughing much of the time. It was hard not to like these two knuckleheads.

The June heat was oppressive with an endless hot, dry, west wind. It didn't cool off much at night and the wind blew relentlessly through the dark. I had not seen a summer like this. The Clear Fork of the Brazos was barely a creek to step across. The trail farther north was wider and not so dusty, but the grass was suffering from the heat and lack of rain. The Prairie Dog Fork of the Brazos was sand bars and puddles. The Pease River at Vernon was nothing but isolated pools of undrinkable water.

Mr. Doan warned us there would likely be shortages of water and grass in the Nations. At least he hadn't heard of any Indian troubles. There had been a few herds ahead of us on the trail. We had gotten a late start this year. I hoped it wasn't too late. Kelly picked up some tobacco for his steady habit. All of us but the little boys had a beer or two and prepared to cross the Red.

The usually boisterous muddy Red River was only ankle deep. We let all the stock fill up. It might be their last drink for a few miles.

"Pecos, I got a bad feeling about this trip. What's your Injun blood tellin' ya?"

"Boss, my Injun blood tells me it's gonna be a long hot trip. My white man blood says we gotta get these damn cows to Dodge."

———————

We pushed the cows a little harder than usual to log fifteen miles. We kept them moving and didn't let them stop to graze. We weren't going to put any fat on them, but we had to get them out of this hot dry part of the country. Maybe there would be better grass and water farther north. The grass where we bedded the cattle was dry and had been trampled by previous herds, but there was enough forage to fill them up.

I rode ahead to the North Fork of the Red River with all the canteens. It was a hot long ride. I found a small area where the water was clean enough for men to drink and filled the canteens. I scouted down the river and found a place a quarter mile down the river where there would be enough water for the stock.

The cattle had filled earlier in the day, but the faster pace, heat and wind had increased their thirst. They were restless and lowed for a drink. After midnight, they finally gave up and bedded down.

The next day we started before it was quite so hot. The cattle had their heads down and were sulky and slow. We had to push them hard. Our canteens ran dry and had to be replenished in the chuck wagon water barrels. The dry conditions raised a column of dust over the herd like the pillar of cloud that guided the Children of Israel to the Promised Land.

As we approached the river, the west wind masked the scent of the water to the north. We veered the cattle a ways east of the trail to direct them toward the water hole on the river. As they got close, the scent of the water filled their nostrils. They threw their heads up and began to moo hoarsely and trot for the river. There was no point in holding them back. They were down the bank and spread out all down the edge of the muddy water drinking their fill.

We made camp there on the river bank and let the cattle graze in the poor brushy scrub. It gave them something to nibble on. We took the horses and mules across the river to a patch of better grazing. Kelly and Jake filled all the water barrels and canteens upstream in the cleaner water. The cook wagon and all five freight wagons carried four thirty gallon cypress water barrels.

Kirby came running up, screaming as he ran. "Aaron! Aaron! Rattlesnake got Tyler!" Running as fast as I could, I found that Kirby had killed a five foot diamondback rattlesnake. Kyle was crouched on the ground holding Tyler's head on his chaps, fang marks clearly visible two inches apart on the side of Tyler's neck.

He looked up with terror in his eyes. "Bury me next to my brother." His breathing came in ragged gasps. His face was gray and swollen. In fifteen agonizing minutes, he was dead.

"He was puttin' hobbles on one of the mules when that snake got him. I never heard it rattle. It just bit him right in the neck and killed him." Tears rolled down Kirby's dirty face.

Nobody in camp felt like eating, so Kelly made coffee and passed around jerky and hard tack. Kirby helped me wash Tyler's body and wrap him in the blanket from his bedroll. We shifted things around in the chuck wagon where we could lay his body. It was a sad quiet night in camp as the hot wind howled.

We hitched two of the wagons together and double teamed the mules. Kelly was the only driver expert enough to handle an eight mule team, so we put him on the doubled rig and moved Kirby to the chuck wagon. There was no excitement in the voices as the wagons started across the shallow river bed, or as Little Jake threw the horses on the trail behind the wagons. The cattle were not especially fond of the poor grazing there and seemed eager enough to head north to find better groceries.

I scouted ahead to Comanche Springs. It was a beautiful place I dreaded with a passion. Big Elk Creek had plenty of water. The huge grassland spreading out to the west was not lush, but it was a dull green. At least it was a lot better than what we had seen so far. The graves of Tate Cooper and Tanner Beasley stood in silence beside the creek. I dismounted the big bay horse, loosened his cinch and waited in the shade of a small grove of cottonwoods. Tyler's death and the graves standing in the sun reminded me how fleeting life could be.

The dust announced the approach of the herd before it arrived. The livestock waded out into the sweet, cool water and drank their fill. Without any encouragement from us, they walked out into the good grass, put their heads down and started eating.

We worked the wagons into a defensive position along the creek, then loose-herded the horses and mules on the grass. All the water barrels and canteens were refilled. Kelly fixed a big supper to make up for the light meal the night before.

Without directions from anyone, Matt and Jake pulled shovels out of holders on the side of the wagon and dug a grave in the dark dry soil next to Tanner. Pecos, Kyle, Kelly and I carried our blanket wrapped friend and laid him in the ground. Jake and Matt played "Shall We Gather at the River." We joined in with subdued voices and repressed tears.

By the time we reached Soldier Springs with its shade and waterfall, the hands at least felt like bathing, and their appetites certainly had returned. But the shadow of gloom still lingered. No one went swimming or jumping off the waterfall. Tyler's death had been a complete accident. That snake could have killed any of us, and there wasn't anything that could have been done to predict or prevent what had happened. I sat by myself after supper leaning against the trunk of the lonely cottonwood tree and smoked my pipe. I had really liked that kid. He had been with us long enough for him to feel like he belonged, especially since he lived and worked on the ranch. But I didn't feel the nagging sense of guilt I had felt after the skirmish with the Cheyenne. Pecos walked over and sat down to me.

"You thinkin' about Tyler?"

"Yeah. Am I that easy to read?"

"Boss, I've known you since you was twelve. We've been friends for sixteen years. You go through the war with a man, ride the river with him as long as we have, you kinda get to know him. I've been thinkin' about him, too. Don't forget he and I lived in that dugout together for the last year. He was a good boy. I'm gonna miss him."

The oppressive heat continued as we pushed north to the Washita. It pulled the water out of our bodies, and seemed to suck the life out of everything alive. The river was so low, we had to go downstream a way to find decent water. The grass was dry and thin. The cattle licked up what they could before bedding down at night, too tired to move.

As at Fort Griffin, the garrison was gone at Fort Supply, and the fort abandoned. The store keeper said the early herds had hard luck with water and grass, too. He placed a small order for supplies for his store from Dodge. The saloon had closed.

Kelly was able to buy green beans, yellow squash and roasting ears at one of the local farms. Little Jake and Zach went picking blackberries. They got enough for a big cobbler and enough chiggers to infect a whole army.

We crossed the North Fork of the Canadian River where it joins Beaver Creek. The cows didn't even get their tails wet.

Soon after crossing, huge thunderheads appeared in the west. There was a scent of rain on the wind, which now carried a definite breath of humidity. Like gathering armies, the towering clouds moved together forming a solid line sweeping in from the southwest. We could see lightning in the clouds flashing across the storm and crashing to the ground. The front rushed toward us, cold air now spilling down from the tops of the angry clouds.

The rain came in huge fat drops, then in almost solid sheets of rain. We kept the herd moving slowly, their hides soaked to the bone. The dry prairie around us soaked up every drop until it could hold no more. The rain continued to pour down until there was water standing on the ground two inches deep. As quickly as the storm had swept down on us, it moved on to the northeast. The sun weakly appeared through broken clouds.

The wagons were now cutting ruts in the road, so I decided to call it a day. There weren't any complaints from the cattle or the cowboys. Once camp was set, they built a big fire away from the cooking fire to dry their clothes. It would be unthinkable to invade the cook's sacred space. Pecos passed around bottles of Neat's foot oil and old rags to wipe down the saddles, boots and chaps. The felt hats, once stiff with caked sweat and dust, sagged like pitiful small umbrellas. The hands pulled some spare tarps off the wagons to lay on the ground to have a dry place to sit and roll out their beds.

The summer sun quickly dried out the trail and we were raising a faint cloud of dust by the next afternoon. The grass looked fresher already.

The fickle Cimarron River posed a problem. The rain had not created a great deal of run-off, but had channeled enough water into the riverbed to create the worst quicksand any of us had ever seen. I tried to test the crossing on the big sorrel horse I was riding, but he was bogging in the sucking mud. I barely got him back to the bank. The quicksand ran in a narrow band, not over fifty feet wide. But it would present an impassable obstacle. A search up and down stream didn't offer anything better. The water would have to be considerably deeper to swim the stock over or wait for the quicksand to dry enough on the top to cross. Neither was going to work. The Deep Hole Crossing on the Cimarron was just deep mud.

I motioned for Matt and Pecos to ride up to the double-hitched wagon Kelly was driving to talk to me. Each one offered some suggestions. We rejected all of them.

Pecos smiled. "I got an idea. Aaron, you remember when we was in Georgia with Uncle Joe and come up on that place where the roads was so swampy we couldn't get through? They had us cut down trees to build a corduroy road."

"That was mighty hard sorry work in the mud and mosquitoes. You think we could do something like that here?"

"There's enough of us and enough trees. We ain't goin' anywhere any other way I can think of."

We picked two cottonwood trees about a foot in diameter that we thought we could manage and turned the boys loose on them with axes. Their young backs and the sharp steel had them on the ground and trimmed of branches in no time.

We fastened a chain around the first trunk and hitched it to a pair of mules. We had the mules pull the logs right to the edge of the quicksand. We exchanged the chains for one inch manila rope, wrapped and tied securely to the river end of the logs.

"Keenan, I want you to try to run across the quick sand to the other side of the river carrying this rope. You're the lightest one. If you get stuck, we'll pull you out with the rope. Think you can do it?"

"Do cow pies stink? Shoot, I bet I can." He pulled off his boots and the dirtiest pair of socks I have ever seen. "I been aimin' to wash 'em."

Grabbing the rough end of the stiff rope, Keenan took off at a run. He hardly sank on the top of the slimy muck until he neared the far edge. He sank above his ankles, but struggled a little and turned to raise the rope in triumph. We clapped and cheered for him as we let out slack for the rope.

"Okay, you little swamp rat. Take a turn around that smooth bark cottonwood tree there by the side of the crossin'." He pulled the rope around the trunk, back to the edge of the seam of quicksand and pulled up all the slack.

"Alright. Head back this way."

He skittered across the top of the quicksand like a water spider. Just as he was about to clear the slime, the rope snagged on a bush. His momentum sent him barreling headfirst into the mud in front of him. He went down with a splash and slid six feet before he stopped. He crawled to his feet and stood dripping black slime.

He erupted with a string of words fitting for the situation, but not suitable for church. The rest of us laughed until we cried.

"Son, if you're able, can you go back, untangle the rope and drag it back? I'll wash your clothes for you myself."

He gamely trotted back across without a stumble, untangled the rope and brought it safely back across the quicksand. He was one tough boy. He was met with our cheers.

Kelly hitched the rope to the waiting mules. "Hup, mules!" They pulled easily away from the river as the slack came off the rope, but dug in when they started to drag a cottonwood log into the quicksand. The tree across the riverbed acted like a crude pulley and drew the log to the other side. "Whoa!"

Keenan had done his duty for the day. I sent Zach to balance himself on the log and loosen the rope. It was very muddy work, but he pulled the right loop on the hitch to release the knot. We pulled the rope back and fastened it to the other log. The mules pulled on the other end of the rope moving the log in the opposite direction. We manhandled the ends until they lay parallel, about twelve feet apart.

The next step involved cutting lots of straight trees, cottonwoods, and post oak, anything straight for at least twelve feet long, and eight inches or more in diameter. These were split in half. The large cottonwood logs were notched just deep enough to accept the crossing half logs. Starting at the south bank we worked our way north to the other side. The question remained whether or not the livestock would cross.

I had Pecos give it a try with his best horse. The stout chestnut gelding tried the first step gingerly. The strange thing didn't bite him, so he stepped right up and crossed at a trot. We doubted any problems with the mules.

An exhausted group of drovers made camp south of the Cimarron. We would try crossing in the morning. The recent rains brought out an army of tree frogs which serenaded us all night with their annoying chirping.

Once breakfast had been cleared away and all the mules hitched, we started across the strange bridge. We sent Kelly with his double-teamed double-wagon first. If anything was going to break through, that would be it. Kelly stood in the wagon seat with his long black whip. "Git up you sorry outfits! Hup, hup!" The mules had crossed wooden bridges many times and didn't hesitate. The cottonwood trunks didn't even sag under the heavy load. He signaled and all the other wagons followed. Little Jake was ready with the horses. They trotted across like they did it every day.

We started the cattle following the horses as they had done every step of this long journey. Matt, Pecos, Kyle and I crowded the front of the column of cattle from both sides, funneling them onto the narrow bridge. The first steer stopped with wood under his feet for the first time, but the crowding of the cattle pressing behind him moved him forward. The hands farther back didn't crowd the cattle, but let them come at a slow walk. The herd crossed in about an hour. Two steers were crowded off into the quicksand. Using the bridge to reach them, they were roped and pulled free. We had succeeded in making the worst river crossing I had ever seen.

―――――――――

We made another five miles that day. We found a bed ground with fresh green grass and clean flowing water in a small creek. The cattle didn't look as good as other herds I had driven into market. They had lost a little weight on the difficult trip. We were only a day's drive from the Arkansas and Dodge City. I decided to hold the cattle here for a week to put on a good fill and gain a little weight, as that would cause them to bring a little more per head than selling as they were now. Keenan took a good scrubbing in the creek. I washed his nasty clothes as I had promised. The socks were beyond saving, so I gave him a spare pair of mine. It didn't seem right that a scrawny teenager who wasn't even shaving yet had feet bigger than mine.

We enjoyed the rest on the good pasture and were blessed with cooler days and gentle breezes. The drovers bathed and swam in the creek. Luke and Levi brought in a fat doe. Kelly fixed fried venison steaks you could cut with a fork, and made a dried apricot cobbler for dessert.

Finally, the cattle had a good bloom on them. We made the distance on to Dodge in an easy drive. A buyer for Joseph McCoy's company came out and offered us thirty-one dollars a head, a dollar above the market.

16

September 11, 1878, Dodge City, Kansas
"All is vanity and striving after wind." Ecclesiastes 1: 14

"COME ON, MR. TURNER. Let's get you and your men paid." This was a new buyer to me for Mr. McCoy, but he seemed a decent sort. "You boys were in the war weren't you?"

"Yes. Army of Tennessee, Patrick Cleburne's Division, Hiram Granbury's Brigade, Texas Fifteenth Regiment of Cavalry, Dismounted, Company K. I was a courier. I left a brother at Camp Stephen Douglas prison in Chicago, but made it back to Texas alive with my other brother, my brother in law, a friend and my captain."

"By thunder, son. I was with the Fourth Iowa. Your regiment drove ours off the road and into the hills at Chickamauga. You boys fought like demons!"

"Well, there was demons enough to go around everywhere. I don't remember the Fourth Iowa scarin' off too easy."

"I'm going to treat you to the usual bath, haircut, shave and dinner from the company. I would be honored if you would let me buy your outfit a drink out of my own pocket after you eat."

"Mr. McClure, I'd be glad to accept as long as the second round's on me." We walked down Front Street together until we reached the huge brick bank. A different banker sat behind the big oak desk.

"Mr. Turner, you probably won't remember me." He stood and shook my hand. "I was your banker in Sedalia, Missouri in 1866, when you brought up a herd from Texas. You were just about fifteen as I recall. My name is Glenn, Danny Glenn. I just worked for the bank in Sedalia, but I bought this one just this year. I'm proud to do business with you again. I hear you've prospered in the Texas cattle business."

"You know, I do remember you. You was pretty decent for a Yankee. You convinced me to try wire transferrin' money to Texas. Well, I don't know about prosperous, but we've got a nice ranch under fence in Callahan County. I usually have five or six hundred head for the market every year and drive up another thousand or so for other folks."

I drew out the hands' wages in silver and plenty for travelling money. The rest was wired to The Cattleman's Bank in Waco. There wasn't a closer bank yet, but I heard rumors when the railroad came through we would see banks coming, too. Our trail crew and teamsters filled the front porch of the bank. The Dodge Marshall had already been by to collect our guns. None were allowed north of the tracks. We could pick up our guns at his office if we left town or went south of the line.

As was our habit, we visited the Chinese bath house and laundry, courtesy of the McCoy Company. I scrubbed extra hard, perhaps in an effort to remove the stain of the three deaths we had suffered the last two years on the trail. The hot soapy water eased the tension from my shoulders and neck. The shampoo and haircut were needed almost as much as the shave. When my clothes, boots, and hat were returned, all freshly cleaned, ironed, brushed and polished, I dressed and joined the others outside the partitions.

Kelly and all the youngsters went shopping with me. Denim pants, shirts, boots, hats and spurs flew across the counter. I found a dress coat, slacks, and a nice shirt to wear for the wedding. The salesman tried to talk me into buying a derby hat. He insisted I try in on in front of a mirror.

Keenan couldn't stand it. He was laughing so hard he about fell over. "You look like one of them tin horn gamblers from Fort Griffin!"

I handed the hat back to the salesman. "No thanks. My young friend here needs to buy some extra drawers and a pair of pants. He decided to drink water out of the Pease River."

I bought Mother a couple of dresses, one that was extra fancy for the wedding. I felt obligated to buy a pretty dress for Alice. Maybe it would improve her disposition, but it seemed like putting jewelry on a hog.

I sold two freight wagons and teams. I had fewer customers on the trail since Fort Supply had dried up. Mrs. Nixon was going to sell out in Fort Griffin and open a little restaurant in Belle Plain. We had agreed the Nixon boys could work for me.

We all met for the free lunch we had been provided. A huge ham graced the table with sweet potatoes, green beans, squash and yeast rolls. It was delicious. Then the waiter brought out real chocolate cake and ice cream, with enough coffee to float a steamboat.

As we were lingering over our coffee, a powerful, awful smell came floating up from somewhere beneath the table. It singed the hair in my nose and made my eyes burn.

With a guilty grin, Keenan jumped up. "Excuse me. I gotta go."

Kirby held his nose. "I think you already did."

———————————

We drifted on down to the Longbranch to meet Mr. McClure, the cattle buyer, and Mr. Glenn, the banker, for drinks. We all lined up at the long polished bar from Kelly down to Keenan. They were waiting for us when we got there. The place was pretty well empty. There was a bored looking gambler playing solitaire at a table in the corner and a rather large bartender.

McClure waved for the bartender's attention. "Set 'em up on me. Anything they want."

I gave Keenan the evil eye. "The four young 'uns will have sasparilla. I hear you got cold beer?"

"Yeah. We got an ice house. Ship it in here in big blocks from up north. We keep the beer kegs on ice and chill the mugs, too. I guarantee it's the coldest beer you can get in Dodge."

"Sounds good." The others nodded their agreement.

McClure held up his sweating heavy mug, thick with foam. "To my Confederate friends." We all drank to that.

Kelly offered "To our Yankee friends."

I lifted up off my elbows and raised my half-full mug. "To General Joseph Johnston, our Uncle Joe."

Kelly was in an unusually festive mood for him. "To General Sterling Price."

Pecos got a serious look on his face. "To the finest field officer in the war, Captain Benjamin Tyus, and Company F."

"Mr. Glenn, did you serve?"

"Yes. I served with the Union troops from Missouri at Prairie Grove and Pea Ridge."

"I was across the line from ya at both places. Got our tail feathers scorched good, too." Kelly grinned.

"Bartender, we're all about dried out here. The second round is on me." He got us all served. The younger boys went over to play billiards. Kelly, Pecos and I remained at the bar with our hosts, while the rest started a small stakes poker game in which the gambler showed no interest.

"Aaron, I was tellin' Danny here about your ranch in Texas being fenced, watered with windmills, and stocked with fine cross-bred cows and pure bred bulls."

"Our operation was just a greasy sack outfit when we started, wasn't it, Pecos."

"You, me, your brother and Shelby was bustin' mavericks out of the canebrakes and river bottoms. It was hard work. We come a long way since then."

"I been runnin' chuck for ya since '66, too."

"You was old, ugly, bald and toothless back then, too."

"Pecos, one of these days I'm gonna fix your grub up real special." We all laughed because we knew he meant it.

"Well, if you Billy Yanks don't mind, we got stuff to do. Thanks for the drinks." We shook hands, gathered up the rest of the crew and hit the swinging doors. Pecos, Matt, Luke and Levi wasted no time in heading to the Marshall's office to get their guns and head to the south side of the tracks. Maybe it was early enough in the day they wouldn't get in too much trouble. Pecos saw me frowning.

"Boss, them Carter boys are both past twenty years old. I'll keep an eye on 'em. It's time you cut the apron strings."

I went to the tobacco shop to stock up on their special number seven pipe tobacco blend. I bought four bottles of French champagne for the wedding. The clerk gave me instructions on how to get it home and how to serve it.

Kelly and Kyle rode herd on the youngsters.

"Kyle, you're not goin' with Pecos' crew?"

"Naw, Biscuit, I got me a sweetheart back home. I don't need no trouble." Kyle was smitten with Cheyenne Boedeker, and the feeling was mutual.

After spending the shank of the afternoon prowling Dodge, we ate at a half decent chili house, gathered our youngsters, horses and guns and rode across the bridge back to camp just about dark.

———

Sometime well after midnight, I heard horses galloping across the bridge, the hoof beats shattering the still night air. Pecos, Matt, Luke and Levi reined up and tied their still saddled horses to the picket line and jumped in their bedrolls. Something sure wasn't right.

About that time, a lone rider approached on horseback. "I'm United States Marshal for Western Kansas, Jess Wayne Webb. Who's in charge here?"

"I'm in charge! Who the hell do you think you are to come gallopin' into a man's camp in the middle of the night without askin' permission? You coulda got yourself shot, Sheriff!"

"I told you my name is Jess Wayne Webb, United States Marshal. Who the hell are you?"

"I remember you, Sheriff. We had some dealin's with you back in Abilene. What brings you out here bustin' into my camp in the middle of the night?"

"You never did identify yourself?"

"I don't like havin' to look up at a man on horseback who's talkin' to me like a horse thief. Get down off your high horse and we'll talk."

"This is your last warnin'! Identify yourself!"

"You gonna shoot a man for not tellin' his name to a rude son of a buck like you? My name is Aaron Turner of Callahan County, Texas. You knowed all along who I am." The camp broke out in laughter behind me. "Am I wanted for murder or somethin'? Climb down and we'll pour you some coffee."

Ignoring my offer of hospitality and the unwritten rules of range etiquette, and taking himself pretty seriously, the lawman stayed on his horse and pushed on with his questioning. "I'm lookin' for four Texans. They busted up a saloon claimin' they was bein' cheated at the roulette wheel."

"Well, let's look around here. Keenan, you and Kirby get up. Did you bust up a bar?"

"Heck, no, Sheriff. We ate at a chili parlor and come home." Keenan added emphasis by loudly passing gas. "You got one you need us to bust up for ya?"

"Kyle, you bust up a bar?"

"Nope. I was with y'all all night."

"You know, I bet it was Little Jake. Wake him up."

The sleepy eleven year old stood up in his droopy drawers, rubbing his eyes. "What do y'all want? I was sleepin'."

"Sheriff, I don't think it was him. Jake, Kelly, did y'all start any trouble at a bar?"

"Nope." Jake yawned.

"I remember you. You're that same Yankee lawman gave us trouble over at Abilene. I bet Joseph McCoy is gonna have somethin' to say about this." Kelly drew himself up to his full six foot eight inches and spat tobacco juice squarely on the toe of the marshal's right boot.

I stepped behind the wagon to light my pipe and got Pecos' attention. "The four of you ride like thunder to get a hold of that cattle buyer and the banker, too."

They untied their saddled horses, slipped off to the south in the dark, before circling back and swimming their horses across the Arkansas. Once across unnoticed, they headed into Dodge. The clerk at the Dodge House remembered them and told them where to find Mr. McClure and Mr. Glenn.

I stepped back near the fire. "We drove fifty-two thousand dollars worth of cattle all the way from Texas to sell in Dodge. I bought three wagon loads of freight to take back. Is this how you treat businessmen? You got a way of pickin' on the wrong folks. I'm gettin' kinda tired of you."

Horses were galloping across the bridge, four riders and a buggy carrying two men. Mr. Glenn got out of the buggy like he was ready to whip someone. "So, Marshal Webb, you had so much trouble handlin' drovers in Abilene, they sent you west to Dodge. Now you're aggravatin' one of the most prominent cattleman that comes to Dodge every year!"

Mr. McClure was so angry he was shaking. We could hear the edge in his voice. "I've already sent a telegram to Mr. McCoy in Abilene. He wired back that he is contacting the Kansas Attorney General to deal with this foolishness."

"Mr. McClure, they said four Texans broke up a bar for gettin' cheated at roulette. They're the only Texans in town right now."

Mr. Glenn got right up to the marshal, who still sat on his horse. "You get down off that horse to talk to your betters." The marshal looked hurt and embarrassed, but got off his horse.

"I'm sorry. I forgot my manners."

"Now, who was it made these allegations?"

"The roulette wheel man, a gambler, and one of the workin' girls."

"So you're takin' the word of the people who were runnin' a crooked game? Maybe that bar needed bustin' up!"

"I guess you could say that. I didn't stop to think about that. They didn't deny they was cheatin' the fellas that busted up the bar."

A lone horseman trotted across the bridge. "Hello the camp. Got a telegram for Marshal Webb." He rode on up to camp, climbed down and handed it to the puzzled lawman. As he stepped under the light of Kelly's lantern, he looked as if he had swallowed a minnow.

Mr. McClure spoke up. "I believe that telegram may pertain to these gentlemen. Read it for us, Marshal."

"It's from the Attorney General in Topeka. It says I am to cease and desist any effort to delay, question or interfere with Mr. Turner or his men. I'm supposed to report to Topeka within three days." He stepped up on his horse and trotted away in the darkness without saying another word. We listened as his horse crossed the bridge.

"Pecos, you boys chip in and give Mr. Glenn enough money to fix up the bar. We appreciate the help, gentlemen. I believe we're gonna leave as soon as we get shoes on the horses and mules."

––––––––––––

We all had on our yellow slickers in the gentle September rain. The showers followed us all the way from Dodge City to the Deep Hole Crossing on the Cimarron. Thunder rolled in the distance accompanied with sheet lightning. The log corduroy bridge was still there. The rains had slowly soaked into the parched prairie and had not caused the river to rise.

Kelly raised his voice. "I'm goin' across first. No point in all of us gettin' hurt if it's not solid."

"Who's gonna cook if you drown, Biscuit?" Pecos asked with a grin.

"Git outta my way, Injun boy. Hup mules!" He slapped the reins across their broad, wet backs and they trotted safely across. "Looks solid. Let's go!"

Kirby's wagon came next. He cracked his long black whip with words he didn't learn in Sunday school. The mules hesitated, then trotted across.

The irrepressible Keenan stood in the wagon box and creatively cussed each mule by name and popped his whip like a pistol. The mules responded like champions and charged onto the make-shift log bridge, thundering their way across to the middle. There they came to a crashing halt.

The top logs on the left side of the bridge had separated and the left rear wheel had dropped into the gap. No amount of urging would move the wagon. It was stuck with a load of barbed wire and groceries.

Kirby parked his wagon and set the brake. He undid the master hitch pin and backed his four mules to his brother's team. A little fiddling with the rigging had all eight mules hitched together. Grabbing the bridle of the right front mule, Kirby urged them forward as Keenan applied the whip.

The mules pulled and strained. The wheel rose slightly, but was too tightly wedged to go anywhere. Kelly backed his team, our best four mules, to the front of Kirby's team. With all twelve mules pulling, the wagon rose half way from the gap, but would go no further.

Zach and Kyle showed up dragging a long straight oak trunk about four inches in diameter. They wedged it under the back axle, then grabbed the far end of the trunk. Kyle hollered, "Try it now!" As the power of the mules engaged the back wheel, it rose again about half way out of its trap. Then Kyle and Zach levered the axle up by pushing down on the oak log. The wagon rose, but didn't quite clear the hole. Seeing the opportunity, Luke and Levi jumped down from their horses and added their strength to the log. With a creak and a groan, the wagon wheel broke free and the twelve mule hitch rolled it to the other side of the Cimarron. The sudden absence of the axle sent all four men tumbling in a heap on the muddy bridge. A loud cheer rose from the whole crew.

We got the rest of the horses and gear across. We were so tired, we made camp right there near the south bank of the river. In appreciation for their extra hard work, I dug in one of the wagons until I found a case of bonded whiskey. It was shared to everyone after supper. Even Kirby grabbed a snort. "Whew! That kicks like a mule and burns all the way down. Mamma sure would be mad."

Taking a long pull from the bottle, fourteen year old Keenan winked at his big brother, "She ain't here right now is she?"

—————————

We passed the North Fork of the Canadian and arrived at the withered up ghost town still known as Fort Supply. The store keeper bought some trade goods for his diminished store. There had been some cowboys pass earlier heading back down the trail, but no news or gossip to pass along. Kelly was able to buy some fresh vegetables and four young roosters. We had fried chicken, biscuits, gravy and sides of black-eyed peas, squash and mashed potatoes. It was better than the Dodge House.

Pecos dug deep into a bowl of blackberry cobbler Kelly served him. The first bite brought gagging, hacking and spitting. "Good night, Biscuit, what did you put in there?"

"Well, I tried a little experiment. I guess quinine don't good in cobbler, Injun boy."

Continuing south, we camped south of the Washita. The rains had brought the parched prairie back to life. The grass was dark green and growing thick and lush. Wildflowers were scattered through the new grass.

Soldier Springs was mighty pretty, too. Big Elk Creek ran full and slightly mud stained. Levi climbed above the waterfall and jumped feet first into the deep pool at its base. The others followed his example and soon joined him.

"Pecos, bet ya a dollar ya won't jump in." Matt goaded him.

"I'll be right behind ya, big mouth."

The two climbed up the red sandstone in their summer drawers and joined the others. Matt went first and made an enormous splash, followed immediately by Pecos.

"Aaron, I'll betcha the dollar I won from Matt that you won't jump."

"I'm the trail boss; I'm supposed to be serious. I got five dollars says I'll do it. You got five dollars left after Dodge City?"

"You're on, Boss."

I climbed the red bluff above the waterfall, but I continued climbing until I was a good twenty feet higher than the place from which the others jumped. Hollering the Rebel yell, I jumped and went far down into the swirling cool deep water. The others followed my lead and started jumping from the higher ledge.

Kelly waded out into the water in his long drawers, sat down and started taking a bath.

"That outta kill all the fish for ten miles downstream." Levi crowed.

"Boy, you shut up, or I'll spit tobacco juice in your chili."

Pretty soon they all joined Kelly and passed around the lye soap. We were all starting to look a little better. After supper, Jake and Kirby got down their fiddles, and Matt joined them with his guitar. They played and we sang until after midnight.

The next day took us south to Comanche Springs on Big Elk Creek. We paid our respects at the three lonely graves.

"Aaron, I never have liked this place. Spirits walk here at night."

"I know, Pecos, I feel it, too."

A lone wolf stood silhouetted on the top of the bluff in the light of the rising moon, howling to unseen companions. It gave me goose bumps. None of us slept well that night.

We made it to the North Fork of the Red River. Once we had crossed, it wasn't far to Texas. We were all ready to get home. I wanted to see Moon and her colt, and head to Groesbeck and see Ella.

Doan's Crossing and Store meant we were back on the sacred soil of Texas. Mr. Doan bought a lot of my freight. I guess he did a steady business.

The Pease River, Seymour, Throckmorton and Fort Griffin passed quickly. I sold the rest of my freight in Belle Plain, except for what we reserved for our own use. From Belle Plain, it was only six miles to home. We left our friends behind there. Pecos and I were ready to get home. We kept the mules at a quick trot. I was finally home. But it wouldn't be complete until Ella was there with me.

17

October 10, 1878, Groesbeck, Limestone County, Texas
Ella

THE CROWING OF MOTHER'S Rhode Island Red rooster heralded the lightening skies in the pre-dawn stillness of the house where I had been born. I dressed and watched a glorious sunrise through the east facing window at the end of the hall. The glowing colors spread slowly across the autumn sky. I had the whole house to myself.

I saddled Sam Houston, the fine stallion I had been given by Chance, in the barn behind the house. "Mornin' Pecos. You sure coulda stayed in the house last night. Wanna go over to my brother's and get some breakfast?"

"I slept fine out here. I didn't wanna have to move my stuff out tonight so you and Ella wouldn't be disturbed. And yes, let's go eat." He stood up from his bedroll. "Oh, my head! You were the only one that stayed sober last night. I feel like I got kicked by a mule."

"Well, are you gonna gripe about it or eat and get some coffee to make it better?"

"Right behind ya, Boss." He had fallen asleep in all his clothes, including his boots and hat. He splashed some water on his face from the water trough and saddled his horse.

"Momma, how about some more pancakes and another cup of coffee?"

"Tryin' to keep your strength up for tonight?"

Glynna shot an elbow so hard in Marcus' ribs he sloshed coffee on himself. "Marcus King! And your own mother sittin' right here. Where's your manners?"

I changed the subject quickly, "Momma, thanks for lettin' us have the house tonight."

"It wouldn't be fittin' for all of us to be there together, now would it? When your daddy and I got married in Georgia, we had to come back to my little house with three children. You and Pecos better show up at the church early, scrubbed and shined. That preacher said two o'clock, not two fifteen. Pecos, are you going to shave? You look like something the cats dragged up."

"Yes ma'am. I'm gonna go to the barber and get a haircut and shave with Aaron."

"Son, your brother Lucius' widow, Ilene, is coming up all the way from Gatesville."

"That's a long trip. I hope she's got somebody to drive her in a buggy. She's a sweetheart."

"Captain and Mrs. Tyus got into Groesbeck last night. They came all this way for your wedding."

"Momma, that's a three day trip. I can't believe they came all that way."

"He thinks a lot of you, son. The captain and you have a long history together; the same with you, Pecos."

"That's all that's left of our company from the war, except Noah. We don't even know where he is, or if he's even still alive. I'd give anything to have him here today."

"Ella's mother is standing up with her."

"Yes ma'am. Did you know her maiden name is Mounts?"

"Seems like she told me that. Where are her people from?"

"Olive."

"Olive? I never heard of that."

"Oh sure you have. Everybody has heard of the Mounts of Olive!"

The whole table burst out laughing. Pecos spewed coffee out his nose.

Momma wiped the tears from laughing so hard off with the hem of her apron. "I swear son, you remind me a lot of your daddy."

The church bell in the steeple rang twice. The clear baritone voice echoed in the crisp fall afternoon through Groesbeck. That was the signal for Pecos and me to walk in with the preacher. I couldn't believe my eyes. "Pecos, look!"

Captain and Mrs. Tyus sat in the pews as I had expected. But the whole Dawson family, all the Shepards, Carters, Webbs, and Nixons were there. They had put together a little wagon train and travelled together to attend my wedding. Someone had even brought Zach Barton. I guessed Belle Plain must be about empty. It suddenly hit me how much these people thought of me. I was excited and humbled.

Glynna was playing the pump organ. As the notes wheezed out, the same preacher who had baptized me said "All rise."

The double doors to the front of the church opened. The sun shone around Ella like an angel whose face I couldn't see. I began to tremble a little. She stepped inside with her parents on each side and the doors closed. Now I could see the prettiest girl in Limestone County. My sweet Ella's smile lit up the whole chapel. They stopped in front of the preacher and the music stopped.

The preacher asked who gave this woman's hand in marriage. Her father, who always had something smart to say, hesitated. He cleared his throat, and wiped his eyes. In a husky voice he croaked "Her mother and I do, Preacher." He gave me her hand. When I touched it, a tingle went down my spine. The preacher droned on, but I could only see and hear Ella.

"Aaron Turner, are you paying attention? Aaron? Do you take Ella to be your lawful wife?"

"Oh. Oh, yes sir, I sure as hell do!" The preacher cleared his throat and rolled his eyes. Pecos and the congregation laughed.

"Ella, do you take Aaron..."

"I do!"

"I wasn't even finished yet, but I guess that will do. Please exchange rings. Repeat after me, Aaron. With this ring I thee wed."

"I do." I don't think that was exactly what I was supposed to say, but Pecos handed me the ring and I fumbled to get it on her hand. The crowd giggled.

"Ella. Repeat after me. With this ring, I thee wed."

"With this ring, I thee wed." Her mother handed her a plain gold band for me and Ella slipped it on my finger.

"Well, at least one of them is paying attention. By the power vested in me as a minister of the Gospel, and by the state of Texas, I now pronounce you man and wife. Aaron, you may kiss your bride."

I laid a good one on her, and wasn't about to turn loose unless she got away. There was lots of stomping and hooting from the crowd.

"Well, I've done many weddings, but this has certainly been the most unusual. I am proud to present to you Mr. and Mrs. Aaron Lloyd Turner." At this, the chapel was filled with hollering, hoots and whistles, and clapping. I grabbed Ella by the arm and proudly escorted her down the aisle.

_____

The women had fixed a big spread of desserts for us with a white wedding cake and a huge bowl of punch. I'm not sure who had done it, but the punch had been spiked at least once and carried a double barreled blast. We moved over to the Fisher's house for a big dance. Matt, Jake and Kirby played and Kelly called the tunes.

Finally, Ella and I drove mother's buggy with Sam Houston tied on behind to her house. Pecos had followed us there and took care of the buggy and livestock. "Don't mind me. I'm staying in the barn." He said with a huge grin.

Our evening began as a honeymoon should until about midnight. All the family, guests and neighbors surrounded the cabin banging pots and pans. "What the cat hair is that racket?"

"Oh, a shiveree! I haven't seen one in years!" Ella squealed with delight. "They won't leave until we give them some little gift or candy."

On the dresser stood a large sack of peppermint candy from Marcus' store. Ella and I began throwing it out the windows to the revelers below. Jake, Kirby and Matt played a sweet serenade as the others sang along. It was nice I suppose, but I was glad when they were gone.

Mother and Alice would not hear of moving with us to the ranch. She gave us a bedroom set, an extra table and four chairs, a pie safe, and a nice set of pots and pans. Ella's mother had made us a special friendship quilt to which all of our family and friends had contributed a block with their names embroidered on it. She also gave us two goose down pillows, three cut glass kerosene lamps, and a large assortment of cooking and eating utensils. The Tyus' gave us a coffee mill. There were too many other gifts to mention.

I carefully loaded everything in the wagon and tied Sam Houston on behind. Pecos rode along with us, but at night made his bed out a respectable distance away.

────────────

When we returned home, we found Luke and Levi had planted rose bushes in the yard. The Webbs had given us a bred sow that resided in the pen near the barn, and the Dawsons had left a flock of Rhode Island hens and a young rooster. There was bacon and ham in the smoke house with a note from the Shepards. Kirby and Keenan had taken it upon themselves to paint the outhouse white, both inside and out.

I took Ella out to meet Moon and General Johnston, who we still called Uncle Joe. Both took an instant liking to their new mistress.

We had many friends and began the first of many happy days in our home together. Over the years, our life together was to be blessed with much peace and joy.

18

Spring 1879, Turner Ranch, Callahan County, Texas
Putting down roots

"AARON, WHAT HAVE YOU and the boys got planned today?"

"Another cup of coffee with you." I had been married long enough to know this was a loaded question.

"Don't you have some ranch work? If you don't, I've got a whole list of things that need doing around here."

"Well, if you'll jot 'em down for me, I'll try to get to them as I have extra time. I'm drivin' the wagon over to the dugout. Pecos and I are takin' the knuckle head brothers to cut cedar posts."

"I'll swear that Kirby is quiet as a tomb, but Keenan is a real firecracker."

"Darlin', you don't know the half of it."

I milked the cow and turned in the calf to get the leavin's. The mules weren't too excited about another day in the sun, but I got them harnessed and headed along the creek to the dugout.

Everyone was up and ready when I got there. The boys lived with Pecos at the dugout Monday morning until Friday night. They rode home after work on Fridays to see their momma at Belle Plain, went to church on Sunday, and rode back for work early Monday morning. They were hard workers and Pecos got along with them pretty well.

I put the boys in the wagon, and Pecos and I rode along on horseback. "You boys alright this mornin'?"

"Yessir."

Keenan passed some outrageously loud gas. "I am now, Boss."

———————

We rolled into the cedar thicket, flushing out a couple of deer. I set the boys to cutting cedar trees while Pecos and I picked out some that would be suitable for corner and brace posts, and tall gate posts.

The axes and saws did their work. The branches were stripped and the bark peeled off, then the posts were stacked in the wagon.

"What'd Miss Ella send for lunch?" A hungry dirty faced Kirby inquired.

"Biscuits and bacon, same as every day. If you want roast turkey, you better get yourself a wife."

"I ain't that fond of turkey." Pecos grinned.

By late afternoon we had a load of posts laid out a rod apart where we intended to build our next quarter mile of fence. We got back to the dugout about four. Keenan and Kirby both stripped off their dirty clothes and went swimming in the creek.

Moon and Uncle Joe trotted up for their usual treat of oats. General Joseph Johnston was two years old and a fine looking colt. "Pecos, this ranch ain't big enough for more than one stud horse. The almanac shows the signs are right and it's too early for flies to be out. What do you say we cut Uncle Joe?"

"Oh, hell. I'd rather take a whippin', but if you're set on doin' it, I'll help."

I used my rawhide rope to throw a hoolihan overhand loop to catch him. He didn't struggle. Pecos used some strong cotton rope and rigged it to cause Joe to lie down. Once he did, we completed securing his feet where he couldn't kick us. Pecos held the rope while I washed and cleaned the area a little. I had an especially sharp blade on my pocket knife I reserved for this type work. He squealed in pain as I made the first cut. I worked quickly to remove the testicle and cord. I used clean pliers to crush the cord and cut just below the crushed area. It broke my heart to hear him groan in pain. I had done this plenty of times before, and finished the other side in no time. I smeared the raw flesh with axle grease. Pecos eased the ropes off of him. He lay groaning on the ground for a few anxious minutes, but then gingerly got to his feet. I held a halter and lead rope and petted and talked to him as he overcame the trauma we had caused. I led him to a pan of fresh oats and he happily began to eat. I slipped the halter off and stepped away. It had to be done.

The boys had come back from the creek to watch the excitement. "Keenan, do you know why we had to do that?"

"I guess so he won't make babies and to calm him down."

"You're exactly right. And it works just as well on teenage boys."

———————

The next morning when the wagon rolled up at the dugout, we switched the team over to a wagon loaded with barbed wire. The boys gathered up the tools while I checked on Joe. He didn't seem any worse for the wear. I let him out of the corral and into the pasture. If he was going to bleed, he would have done it by now.

When we reached the south boundary of our deeded land, the southeast corner and brace posts were already set, as were the quarter mile brace assemblies. I unrolled enough wire to fasten it to the corner post. The boys slid a four foot piece of pipe in a roll of barbwire and started walking toward the brace post, unrolling the wire as they walked. Pecos and I drove the wagon down to wait for them. Once they arrived, we fastened the wire to the back of the wagon and had the mules ease forward until the slack was out of the wire. We used a crowbar to tighten it further and drove in a few staples. Once it was secured, I wrapped the loose end tightly around the brace post.

The boys both had one rod lengths of chain that they used to locate the proper location for the posts. They would mark it with the heel of their boot and start digging with the posthole diggers. The soil here didn't have too many rocks, so the digging was not especially bad. Once they had the holes forty-two inches deep, they dropped in the post. As they added dirt, they used the flat end of the digging bar to pound the dirt. There was a mark on the digging bar to show where each of the wires should be attached to the post. They drove in a staple and moved to the next post. Pecos and I joined them, working from the other direction toward them. It took all four of us all day to get the quarter mile of posts and one wire up, but it was straight as an arrow.

––––––––

We were all worn out when we got back to the dugout, but I wanted to spend a few minutes working with Uncle Joe. Holding his halter, I let him smell a saddle blanket I had used on his mother. He sniffed and nibbled at it. I tossed it down at his feet. He was a little startled and took a step back and pointed his ears at the offending blanket. He lowered his head and smelled it. I could see the muscles in his neck relax as he recognized the scent. He pushed it around with his nose, but it didn't try to bite him. I repeated the process until he paid no attention to the blanket being dropped. This was enough of a lesson for the day. I rewarded him with a little oats and lots of praise and brushing.

The first step again was to stretch on the first wire to give us a guide to lay out the fence. We spent the entire next day setting out another quarter mile of cedar post and stapling up the bottom wire. I was hot back-breaking, dirty work. The only good part of it was you could see your progress day by day. I would never learn to like building fence.

I worked with Joe a little more, repeating the previous day's lesson without incident. Then I took the blanket and gently rubbed it on his neck, back, rump and legs. He was a little nervous at first, but quickly caught on that the blanket wasn't dangerous. Then, I slowly pulled the blanket from his back up his neck and over his head and face. He didn't even flinch. General Joseph Johnston was one smart horse.

The next morning we began unrolling and stretching more wire on the now half mile of cedar posts. Once each wire was tight as a guitar string, we put up its counter-part on the other side. At that point, we all grabbed staples and hammers and began nailing up the wire. In two days, we had a solid half mile run of sturdy, tight, five strand barbed wire fence.

Joe was beginning to learn about a saddle. I took an older saddle I had used on his mother, and allowed him to sniff and nibble on it. I shook it to make the fitting clank and jangle. He stomped his foot and snorted, but he didn't bolt. Once he was calm again, I dropped the saddle in front of him and stepped back. His curiosity overcame any fear and he nosed around on the saddle and even rolled it over with his nose. Again, we repeated this until he basically ignored it.

We went to work at the southeast corner again, but this time laid out our fencing materials heading north. We got the bottom wire strung to the quarter mile brace and from there to the next one north, a half mile run. We got part of a wagon load of cedar posts set before we played out.

It was Friday night, and Keenan and Kirby bathed in the large tank at the dugout. They put on fresh clothes and headed out to spend Friday, Saturday and Sunday night with their mother in Belle Plain. It was only six miles and the way those two rode, they would be there in an easy hour and a half.

Ella fixed dinner to include Pecos on the weekends. He got tired of bachelor fare at the dugout. She had made a chicken pie with potatoes and carrots with a top crust on it. She also made a dried apple cobbler for dessert and lots of good coffee. She knew Pecos and I liked ours really strong and black, so she made it that way. To hers, she added a little water, a little sugar and cream or milk if we had it. We all sat on the porch while I smoked my pipe. Ella had given up trying to pair Pecos with any of the several pretty single college girls at Belle Plain. Pecos was going to do what he was going to do; there was no pushing him. He rode back to the dugout for the night, as usual.

Ella and I were happy together in our Sears and Roebuck catalogue house above Pecan Bayou. It was home to both of us. We often sat together on the porch and talked until time for bed except in really cold weather. It was a time of day I treasured.

I rode Sam Houston over to the dugout Saturday morning. Pecos and I shared a cup of coffee. We planned to work with the colt a little then go out and work part of the day on the fence. We seldom took Saturdays off from work, but didn't work as hard as we did during the week.

I began with the blanket, and worked up to the saddle. Joe was calm as could be. I gently settled the saddle on his back and led him around the tall corral. The cinches, flank leathers and stirrups flopped against him. He turned his ears and rolled his eyes back to see that it was just the same old saddle he already knew. I pulled the saddle off and on again several times and then treated him to his oats and a brushing. He was learning quickly.

Coming home to Ella always made me smile. She met me at the kitchen door with a hug, kiss and a glass of cool water. I cleaned up while she finished supper.

We had taken up a habit of joining hands and saying a short prayer before we ate. We had done it in my home growing up, although it was Momma who led the prayers. We both prayed, Ella first, then me. We even did this on Friday and Saturday when Pecos was with us. He would bow his head, but never said a prayer that I could hear. Once in a while before we started, he would remind me to pray for one of the neighbors who were hurt or sick, but not often. Pecos had his own relationship with God, and was very private about it. Whatever Ella fixed was good, but I could have eaten burned biscuits and beans with the rocks left in and still have been just as happy.

Pecos usually didn't stay long on Saturday nights. He went back to the dugout and took a bath and shaved. After supper, I helped Ella with the dishes and we sat on the porch and talked, just talked about our day and little things. Sometimes we talked about our frustrations, which were few, or our dreams which were many. I smoked my pipe and enjoyed her company.

"I love the smell of your pipe. I don't know why, but it makes me happy. Sometimes during the day, I'll open your tin of tobacco and think of you. But remember, please, no smoking in the house."

"Yes ma'am. My Momma has the same rule. I'm glad it don't count when I stay out at the bunkhouse." I gave her a dimpled grin.

"That's a good thing, because if you start smoking in the house, you'll be sleeping in the bunkhouse a lot more often."

I goosed her in the ribs. "Ah, Ella, you'd miss me too much for that!"

"Mr. Turner!" She giggled.

I sat and finished my pipe in the cool night air, rocking and holding her hand. I had found peace and happiness with Ella.

————————

Ella planted fruit trees when we moved into the house. They had bloomed and were starting to set tiny green fruit. I built a six foot tall, ten-strand barbed wire fence around her orchard and garden to keep the deer out. I tied chicken wire around the bottom to keep our hens from pecking in the garden and to keep the rabbits out. She loved to make things grow.

I rigged discharge pipes from the windmill storage tank to carry water to the house, garden and barn by opening and closing different brass valves. This was handy to water the garden, fill the water troughs, and especially for water to the house. I wrapped the pipes with a thick layer of old tow sacks and rags, then coated the outside with tar to keep them from freezing. The pipe to the house had a discharge valve in the kitchen sink and in the bathroom. The wood-burning stove had come with an optional water heating tank on the side. It was easy to fill from the top and to empty into a bucket with hot water at the bottom. It was a luxury to be able to take a hot bath most of the time.

I helped hoe the garden if the weeds started to get ahead of Ella, but she preferred to keep her own garden. She planted beautiful flowers around the house and in the garden. She tended the roses the Carter boys had planted like a mother taking care of a baby. She hummed or sang quietly to herself when she worked in the flowers or garden. It made me smile to hear her. She had me rig an extra discharge pipe that would send water to the pecan trees if the weather had been dry.

On Sundays, we hitched up the spring wagon and drove the six miles to church in Belle Plain. The Baptist and Methodist ministers took turns preaching every other week and were careful not to step on each other's toes. It didn't matter a lot one way or the other to me. I just enjoyed the singing, preaching and praying. Ella usually fixed a basket of food of some sort to share with whoever invited us to stay for dinner.

Pecos didn't come much, although he would show up randomly, just often enough to keep us guessing. "Aaron, I believe in God. He is all around us, in the wind, the grass, the water in the creek, the hawks circlin' in the breeze. I talk to Him and I think He hears me. The world He made speaks back to me."

———————

Spring round up arrived with plenty of good slow, steady rains, green grass and a new crop of calves. Since I was a little boy, I had always loved watching calves play. I rode through the pastures twice a day checking for mother cows needing help. Because of their partial longhorn heritage, they had small calves and little trouble. The use of the Hereford bulls gave us babies with white faces. They looked good, weaned heavier and were ready for market at age two, as opposed to four years old for the straight longhorns.

We assembled the crew and separated the market ready steers and a few older cows. They were road branded with the upside down T.

"Best cattle we've taken up the trail, Boss."

"Pecos, you been there with me every step of the way. You get as much credit as I do."

"Naw. You're plenty enough cowboy, nearly as good as me." Pecos grinned. "But you're the cattleman. You know how to make money on 'em. Me, I can do anything you want done to cows, but you're the brains that makes this deal work."

"We've come a long way from bustin' mavericks out of the creek bottoms and cane breaks."

It was fine to eat Kelly's cooking and spend some time with Little Jake. He got to do cow work on horseback until time to help with supper. The little rat was nearly twelve, getting tall like his daddy. I watched him work. He was learning fast and was going to make a hand.

Pecos and Matt had a running competition on roping calves to drag to the branding fire. They were a sight to behold, as they hardly ever missed a loop. Matt's brother, Jake, was giving them a run for their money. It wouldn't be long until he was as good as they were.

Kyle, Zach, Luke and Levi could do anything that needed doing on a ranch, including rope. But few people could match Pecos and Matt. Of course, Levi always had something to say about anything he was doing. That one should be a preacher as much as he could talk.

Kyle had married Cheyenne in March. If he died today, I don't think the undertaker could get the smile off his face. He had claimed homestead land for both of them next to his father's place. It had a quarter section of cropland in cotton, corn and wheat, but he ran cattle on the rest of it.

Zach, Kirby and Keenan had all come a long way. They could all three cut, sort, rope, drag, flank, brand, and castrate. Plus, those Nixon boys had turned into fence building fools. They were good enough that, if we showed them where to start and finish, we could let them do the rest, and it got done right. Zach showed an especially good understanding of horses and was good at training them.

The older hands were lounging in front of the dugout after supper. Keenan carefully climbed along the log holding down the barn tin on the front of the dugout until he was directly above the unsuspecting cowhands. Adjusting his aim for the breeze, Keenan peed on the whole bunch of them. The war was on! He took off running, but Pecos caught him by the feet with a quick loop. They carried him tied up like a hog down to the edge of the creek and took turns dunking him. We all laughed until our sides hurt.

With their experience gained from drilling the first well, the next three went easier. A windmill was placed over each of the new wells and over the old hand-dug well at the dugout. The new wells opened up pasture to grazing that had hardly ever been used due to its distance to water. It increased the carrying capacity of the ranch tremendously. The cable tool walking beam drilling rig worked so well that we hired out to drill for neighbors when we had time. It was nice to make the extra money and to help them improve their place.

The fencing project continued relentlessly until there was a perimeter fence and gates around the entire sixteen sections. It made the job of keeping up with the cattle very easy. The wild longhorns, which had inhabited the land they shared with buffalo when we first arrived, had been replaced by shorter, thicker, faster growing and easier to handle half-whiteface cattle. There were only a few older full-blood longhorn cows left in the herd. The days of gathering unclaimed wild cattle and building a herd had been replaced by owning the land on which our home raised cattle grazed.

19

June, 1879, Turner Ranch, Callahan County, Texas
The Last Drive to Dodge

THE TEXAS AND PACIFIC Railroad was building slowly, relentlessly to the west. If they stayed on schedule, the rails would be in Callahan County the summer of 1880. That would be a blessing when it occurred, but we had a herd to drive to Dodge City. We discussed driving the herd east to meet the tracks, but they had no cattle facilities for a long way east to Fort Worth. They would be building loading pens soon, but there were not there yet. Additionally, due to the cost of the freight on shipping the cattle to Chicago, the price was about five dollars a head less there. Fort Worth was developing shipping pens to handle huge volumes of cattle, but the facilities for slaughtering such numbers of cattle didn't exist west or south of Chicago yet. For now, there was going to be one last drive to Dodge for us.

———

The spring which had started with such promise had turned off dry, very dry. The native grasses which had earlier been green had already gone dormant. The hot wind blew like the doors to hell had been left wide open, sucking the life out of man, beast and anything green. Thankfully, there was plenty of surplus grass left from last year, and there had been some early growth.

We had begun to push cattle out of the western side of the ranch when a little thunderstorm arrived. We heard thunder and saw lightning in the distance. A light sprinkling of rain began to fall, sure nothing to brag about, but at least it was wet.

Zach Barton came galloping up to me. "Boss, look yonder!"

A stray lightning bolt apparently had started a grass fire. Light winds were blowing in the direction of the ranch.

"Leave the cattle! Let's go!"

We galloped to the nearest gate, and headed west for the fire. The smoke was building and the smell was sickening. It made our eyes burn and noses run. We swung north to be able to get in behind the line of flames. Little Jake held the horses. The rest of us stripped off our chaps and used them to attack the fire. The heavy leather slapped down on the flames and extinguished them. The gentle sprinkle and slight winds kept the fire from exploding in the dry grass.

As the storm passed over us, a brisk wind took its place. The fire quickly grew into a wall of flames. It was getting away from us fast.

Pecos ran up to me. "See them two stray longhorns north of us?"

"This ain't the time to be catchin' mavericks!"

"I got an idea. I need Matt. Come on!"

Pecos and Matt grabbed their horses from Little Jake and raced toward the stray cattle. Pecos roped the closest one and Matt caught the second. Without a word of warning, Pecos pulled out his Colt and shot that big brute right between the eyes. Matt looked on in amazement. He jumped of his horse and pulled out his big bowie knife. Quick as a flash he split that carcass right down the breast bone all the way to the rear end. He set the blade right over the middle of the pelvic bone and smashed down with his boot, splitting the steer completely in half. He signaled for Matt to do the same. He pulled his Winchester out of the boot and stepped off his horse and shot the steer he had caught. Pecos came over to help him split it open.

"We're gonna use these to smother out the fire. Ride so the carcass goes directly over the line of the fire. I'm goin' ride right behind the fire line, you come close behind me, swingin' in just a little farther."

Pecos took his horse at a fast trot and swung out just enough that the steer carcass was dragging to his left, right on top of the fire. The huge body smothered the fire as he rode. Matt's pass got anything that Pecos had missed. Behind them were isolated spots that were still burning, but we ran to them and beat them out with our chaps.

They continued to trot down the quarter mile back side of the fire. Pecos made a wide swing, causing the splayed steer carcass to swing sharply now to his right side. He headed back north up what was left of the fire with Matt close behind. We got the few hot spots that were left, and the fire was out. It was one of the most amazing things I had ever seen.

We all gathered back at the horses to get a drink from our canteens. Pecos and Matt retrieved their ropes and rode to us.

"I never see anythin' like that in my life. How'd you know to do that?" I panted.

"I seen my daddy and another man do it once before the war. It didn't work this good, though. Daddy got too close and burned the tail plumb off of his horse." We all started to laugh at what must have been a once in a lifetime sight.

Never being one to waste salvaged meat since the war, Pecos and I cut the hindquarters and back straps off the stinking singed steers. We had butchered out many a horse and mule like this so we could have some fresh meat to eat. Kelly could fix this into a few fine meals. The stray steers had come in handy.

We had six hundred and twenty-three grown steers and barren cows when we drove them over Lytle's Gap to Belle Plain on June 11, 1879. Our friends and neighbors there added another nine hundred and fifty-four head to give us almost eighteen hundred head, our largest herd ever.

"Captain Tyus, I believe these are the best cattle we've ever sent to market."

"Yes, those Hereford bulls really throw fine, fast growing calves. I heard you got your entire ranch enclosed with a barbed wire fence."

"Yessir, and we added some windmills to get better use out of our farther pastures. Ella and I each plan to apply for another section of homestead land adjoining ours when we get back from Dodge. Pecos has already got some on the west side."

"I guess you'll have more fences to build and another well and windmill to install. I'm following your example, Aaron. We've already been cutting posts and setting braces and corners. Could you bring me a load of wire and a gear box and an eight foot Eclipse fan? I'd like to hire you to dig a well for me."

"Well, Cap, you catch on quick."

A light, slow, gentle rain fell every day from Belle Plain until we crossed the Red River at Doan's Store. I had loaded the empty freight wagons with buffalo bones at Ft. Griffin. There weren't any hides and never would be again. There were a few stray buffalo around in the canyons up on the plains, and along the upper reaches of the Brazos, but for all practical purposes, they were forever gone.

The grass was green and growing. We took our time and let the cattle gain a little weight on the trail. We were making about ten miles a day. When we reached Comanche Springs, the cattle were already noticeably fatter. The prairie here was in prime condition. The tall fresh growth of native grass was mixed with wild flowers, burr and yellow sweet clover. We decided to stay a week to really flesh out the cattle, horses and mules. This was as close as it got to livestock heaven.

Luke and Levi brought in a couple of nice fat young deer while we were there, and Keenan and Kirby bagged four jake turkeys. We feasted the whole week.

Kelly moved a little slower and more stiffly than when we had met thirteen years ago. I know he was over sixty. All three of his daughters were married and didn't live too far away. He even had a grandson over at Buffalo Gap.

Kyle Shepard was kind of quiet around camp. He had never been away from his wife before and was homesick for her. Matt had married a girl from the college at Belle Plain. It had been a real big wedding. She was a fine girl and very pretty. They had built a nice limestone cottage with a red tile roof next to the blacksmith shop.

I didn't know if Pecos would ever marry. He got lots of attention at every event in Belle Plain and was considered the most eligible bachelor for miles around. He really soaked up the attention, but mostly he enjoyed his freedom.

The three graves there were a solemn reminder of the fragile and brief nature of life. For now it was wonderful, but I knew it could change in the blink of an eye.

We finally moved on to Soldier Springs, our favorite stop on the trip. We pushed slowly north, crossing the Washita. It didn't present any problems, but found we Ft. Supply to be a ghost town. Kelly was able to buy some fresh vegetables from a farmer there along with milk and eggs. Zach and Little Jake picked wild plums near the river. I ate so much of the cobbler Kelly made for supper, I could hardly move.

Out of curiosity, I had scouted ahead of the herd to the Deep Hole Crossing on the Cimarron. The water was running deep and slow. Not a log remained of the corduroy bridge we had built the previous summer. I suspect they might have caused a nice log jam somewhere down stream. I had never seen more work than we had done to cross a river than there last summer. The crossing would require the cattle to swim, but I didn't find any evidence of the quicksand that had plagued us; the current had scoured it down to a hard riverbed.

When the herd caught up, Kelly started his wagon across first. It wasn't far for the mules to swim. The current was slow, and both banks were gently sloping and firm. The other three wagons had no trouble. Kirby, Keenan, and Zach had made pretty decent teamsters.

It wasn't a long way from the Cimarron to the south bank of the Arkansas River. We had the cattle spread out and grazing in four days of slow travel, fattening a little more each day. These were the best animals I had ever driven north to any market. Demand was good for fat Texas beef.

Mr. McClure was there representing Mr. McCoy's company again. "Aaron, these cattle look like the ones we see that have been fattened on corn. They're carryin' more meat and tallow than any cattle I've seen all summer."

"What are they worth to you?"

"The common stuff comin' up from Texas has been bringin' thirty-two dollars a head. I'll give you thirty-five for these."

I smiled and shook hands with him. It was a money making price. He handed us a bottle of good whiskey and a box of cigars to share with the crew.

We got our banking, bathing, eating and shopping done in one day. I told Keenan to behave himself at dinner. Matt, Pecos, Jake, Luke and Levi were back in camp by dark. They said Dodge City just wasn't as much fun as it used to be. I didn't find out until later that the Marshal had followed them like a bloodhound all over south Dodge until they just gave up and came home.

On the return trip, we had just left Soldier Springs heading south when a thunderstorm blew up like a keg of gun powder. An icy wind rolled off the towering tops of the gray-green wall clouds. A cold rain hit us first, followed by marble sized hail that hit hard enough to hurt both man and beast.

There was no shelter from the storm and no way to out run it. It made sense to just keep pushing on until it passed.

There was a blinding white flash and deafening blast. Lightning had hit right among us. Zach Barton had traded off his wagon driving duties for the day with Kyle. To our horror, he and the horse he was riding lay smoking on the wet ground. The lightning had blown the soles off Zach's boots and the shoes off the horse. With shaking hands, we gathered up his singed body as the storm raged around us. We tearfully and gently laid him in one of the wagons and pushed on south. Keenan and Kirby both had tears streaming down their faces mixed with raindrops. I choked down the hot acid in the back of my throat, as my stomach convulsed at what I had just witnessed.

There was nowhere to run and nowhere to hide, so we doggedly pushed on down the trail. Within fifteen minutes the storm blew on to the southeast. Water-logged sunlight broke through the clouds. Thick fog rose from the ground that was covered three inches deep in hail. The grass was laid flat as if it had been mowed down for hay.

A dry westerly wind began to blow. It gradually dried out our soaked clothes. The trail took us to Comanche Springs. We made camp there that night for what would be the last time, although we didn't realize it at the time. Big Elk Creek was running like a river and the wide prairie looked strange in its battered state.

The ground was soaked, but Matt and Jake dug a grave for Zach next to Tanner and Tyler Beasley and Tate Cooper. They tuned their guitar and fiddles, and Matt, Jake and Kirby played "Shall we Gather at the River" again. For the rest of my life whenever I heard that hymn, my thoughts returned to Comanche Springs and the four friends we had left behind. I spoke a few words and we drove a stake at the head of the muddy grave. For all its natural beauty, I had come to hate this place and hoped I would never return.

———————

"Boys, I made coffee. Here's some jerky and hardtack. I ain't got the stomach for cookin' tonight. I seen too many kids die at this damn place." Kelly pulled out the extra wagon tarps to place under our bedrolls. The ground was just soaked. Even the best bedroll couldn't keep this slop out without the extra tarp.

Kelly brought me a cup of coffee. I couldn't remember him serving me many times before. I took a deep drink and realized why he had personally delivered it. The cup was about half whiskey and half coffee. He knew I needed it.

He did cook us a good breakfast before we got back on the road home, leaving Comanche Springs forever behind us. As far as I know, none of us ever returned, but its ghosts and memories were never far away.

———————

We passed the North Fork of the Red River and pushed the mules south to make it to Doan's Crossing on the Red in one long hard day. We had seen enough of the Nations. I talked to Mr. Doan for a while. He said the railroad was moving west so fast he doubted there would be much traffic here in a year. He was moving his business into Vernon. The buildings would remain behind as silent monuments to what once had been and was soon to be no more.

As we passed Clyde, a man in a buggy stopped us. "You drovers won't have to go to Kansas anymore. The railroad will be in Clyde by spring. They're already building a rail station and loading pens. I reckon this will be your last drive."

We looked at each other. Pecos laughed. "I guess he's right. What are we gonna do for fun every summer?"

20

Spring, 1880, Turner Ranch, Callahan County, Texas
"Will the Circle be Unbroken?" Traditional American Hymn

THE MAN IN THE BUGGY
had been right. The railroad reached Putnam, Baird and Clyde
ahead of schedule. The tracks of the Texas Pacific were almost
to Abilene now. Stores sprang up in each location. Boxcars
unloaded vast quantities of sheet metal, lumber, barbwire,
windmill gears and fans, hardware and groceries of all kinds.

The towers of windmills popped up across the prairie
like giant summer sunflowers. I trained Levi and Luke to run
the cable tool walking beam drilling rig. They were kept busy
every day but Sunday, making money for themselves and me.
Barbed wire now began to surround all the cattle country that
had previously been unfenced. Blooded bulls arrived at the
train stations to upgrade the remaining unimproved herds.

I had always been able to recognize an opportunity
to make a dollar. I contracted to use my freight wagons and
mules to deliver goods from the railheads to the more distant
communities and ranches. Kirby and Keenan each drove a
route, so that the circuit was completed regularly. I applied for,
and won, the contract to carry the mail. It paid fairly well, and
my wagons were going that way regardless. The boys carried
catalogues with them on their routes. People would order the

things they wanted, and when they came in on the train, they delivered them to their door.

Belle Plain and the college grew and prospered. It had been made the county seat, as Captain Tyus had hoped. However, the railroad was six miles to the north. The towns along the railroad were destined to prosper while the others faced an uncertain future at best.

Matt Dawson's blacksmith shop was very successful. He and his wife had a little boy they named Travis. His parents both continued to teach at the college. Jake Dawson homesteaded four sections that joined his parents' and brother's land. He ran the ranch for the family. He married a tall blonde haired girl from the college.

Kyle Shepard and his wife, Cheyenne, had a pretty little girl. He farmed a little land, like his father, and ran cattle on the rest. They had a beautiful farmhouse on a small creek on the road from Belle Plain to Clyde.

Kelly tended a few cows and cooked for the area ranch roundups, but his age and years of hard work had caught up to him. Although he was not as active as in his younger days, he was widely liked and respected in the area. Little Jake was big enough that nearly everyone had dropped the "Little" from his name. He was just Jake Webb. He basically ran the Webb place for his family and helped with the chuck wagon cooking. I don't remember meeting anyone who didn't like Jake.

Luke and Levi stayed busy with the well digging business, but kept their herd of cattle. They couldn't dig wells during calving and branding season. They were engaged to a pair of sisters from Clyde with plans for a fall wedding. Their father still taught at the college. Their family was very active in the little church at Belle Plain.

Keenan and Kirby Nixon worked for my freight business and for the ranch depending on where they were needed. They still lived at the dugout with Pecos Monday through Thursday, but headed to their mother's house in Belle Plain on Friday nights. They were like part of our family.

Pecos worked with me every day. He had taken up land west of mine. We dug a well and put up a windmill in the middle of his four sections. We built a fence all the way around it, tying it in to the fence that already existed between us. He continued to live in the dugout. We shared the cow work equally, and he continued to take his meals with us Friday and Saturday nights.

Late in the first year we had been married, Ella miscarried a tiny baby girl. We had not even announced to anyone that she had been expecting. We kept the loss to ourselves. Only Pecos knew, as he had dug a tiny grave for her in the pecan grove. But Ella conceived again. As the time grew closer, it was noticed she was expecting. Robin Nixon was the closest thing there was to a midwife in the area, and there certainly wasn't a doctor for miles.

Ella's pains came close and strong. I left long enough to send Keenan to Belle Plain to bring his mother back in a hurry in our spring wagon. Kirby and Pecos didn't know what to do, but they kept the fire stoked in the kitchen to keep the water reservoir full and hot. They tended my chores around the place feeding the horses, milking the cow and gathering the eggs. "I ain't never milked a cow before, but I guess I'll do it for Aaron. It don't seem like fittin' cowhand work." Pecos groused.

I sat with Ella and held her hand. I tied soft cotton ropes to the corner posts at the foot of the bed she could pull against when the time came. She had me lay thick towels under her and prop her up with pillows. Just as she felt her water break, and the contractions started much harder, I heard the wheels of a wagon roll into the yard.

Robin had me step out of the room. She called through the closed door, "The baby is comin' head first and everything looks right. Get ready with some clean towels when the baby comes. I need a pan of hot water as quick as you can get it here."

"Here's the water, Aaron." Kirby had heard his mother and brought the water to the door. I took it in to her. By the time I was back to the door, he had the towels.

I could hear Robin urging Ella to push. She must have been bearing down with all her might, as I could hear her groan. "The head is right here now, Ella. One more good push and this baby will be out. Grip those ropes and pull hard while you bear down." There was a mighty loud groan followed by a short scream. I jumped a foot high. But almost immediately, I heard a baby cry. "Aaron, you gotta nice lookin' redheaded little boy."

When I was invited in, Ella was beaming ear to ear, holding a tiny baby to her chest. I turned back the sheet to see my first born son. He was red and wrinkled, and seemed longer than I had expected.

We named the baby Aaron Allinson Turner. This is what we had intended for him to be called, but from the time he was born, everyone called him "Al."

A telegram came from Groesbeck through the lines along the railroad track down the leg to Belle Plain for me. Mother had taken ill and Marcus thought I should come quickly. I saddled up Sam Houston and tied my things on Uncle Joe. I took turns riding them hard, but it still took three days to get to Groesbeck. There wasn't a faster way to get there by train, and there was just so far you could go in a day on a horse without killing them.

Marcus met me at the barn as I unsaddled my horse. "Hello Aaron. I'm glad you could come." He shook hands with me. "Mother is real sick. The doctor says its pneumonia. She had it real bad when I was a kid and she nearly died with it. The doctor says it may have left her lungs weak. I don't know. She's been askin' for you."

"Momma?"

"Son, I'm so glad you're here. Pull a chair over here and sit by the bed where I can talk to you better." She looked so weak, so frail. Her color had a gray cast to it, and I could tell from her labored breathing that her pneumonia was very bad.

"Heard you had a boy. What's his name.?"

"Aaron, like me and my father."

"That's good. He would like that. I'm goin' to see him real soon."

"The baby?"

"No, Aaron. Your father, and David and Lucius. I'm very much ready to go. I've been waiting to see you. I want you to understand that I want to be buried here in Groesbeck. I know your father is buried in Leon County, but there are too many bad memories there. Do you understand?"

"Yes ma'am. Momma, you did so good raisin' us kids by yourself. I love you so much."

"Aaron, I don't know if you'll ever know how much I love you. When you were just a boy, you tried so hard to protect me. When you came home from the war, you just took charge and kept us together, made money selling cattle to pay the taxes and keep us in groceries. I don't know what we would have done without you. I'm real proud of you, my baby boy. You've always been good to me, and you've grown into a fine man. I love you very much."

"Thank you, Momma."

A fit of coughing seized her. She waved me off, she couldn't talk any more. I sat with my sister, Mary Ann, and half-brother, Marcus, at her bedside. Just as the sky started to lighten her east facing window, she took a deep breath, and as she exhaled, it was her last. We buried her in Groesbeck as she had requested.

We sold her place and belongings and gave all the money after the taxes to Alice. She went away to a boarding school in Dallas. We never heard from her or saw her again.

_____

Spring gently arrived with beautiful weather and good rains. The flocks of sand hill cranes that I had come to love came back from their wintering grounds down south. They flew over in irregular, ever-changing patterns. Sometimes they flew in an organized V like geese, but more often they flew in an indescribable shape. Their calls could be heard far before I could see them. They spoke to me of something wild and free. In a way, they reminded me of the vanished buffalo and herds of mustangs and maverick cattle.

It was calving season. Pecos and I rode through the cattle twice a day. We tried to keep the cattle close to the corral in case of trouble.

"Boss, there's one off by herself down by the creek. Let's check it out."

As we approached, the young cow didn't try to get away, didn't try to get up. She only lifted her head and lowed pitifully. Then I saw why.

"Pecos, there's a foot hangin' out. Bet the calf's hung up."

We tied the horses and eased toward the cow. She was a first calf heifer. The foot that was showing looked pretty big. Pecos quickly used a pigging string to tie her front feet. She didn't even struggle. It seemed as if she knew she was in a bad way, or too worn out to fight. She lay on her side with her back legs extended. Pecos slipped a soft cotton rope we carried for this purpose around each back foot and ran the rope in a loop around her neck. She would have considerable movement, but if Pecos had tied her correctly, she wouldn't be able to kick enough to hurt me.

I examined her and found the right leg of the calf was turned under at the knee. I gently reached inside and unfolded the leg until it was out like the left one. With her next contraction a nose appeared, and then a whole little white-faced head. But she wasn't able to push the calf any farther. I grabbed the front legs of the calf and pulled gently. I felt them move slightly forward, then firmly stop.

"It's hip locked. Help me push the calf back in just a little and see if we can turn it."

She tried valiantly to push the calf out again with the same result. When the contraction eased, we both pushed the calf back gently. I took both legs above the knee and rotated the calf ninety degrees until its right foot was under her back bone. The birth canal in a cow is shaped like an oval, with the widest part going up and down. The widest part of the calf is its hips, so by turning the calf, maybe we could help her deliver it. When she contracted again, I braced my feet against her hip bones and pulled as hard as I could. There was a little movement forward, then with a sudden release, a huge bull calf slid out on top of me.

Pecos rolled the calf off me and cleaned the nose and mouth. The calf still didn't breathe. He grabbed a long stem of dried grass and tickled inside the calf's nose. He sneezed! And with the sneeze came several deep breaths. The calf's dark brown eyes were open and beginning to shine. I grabbed an old towel from my saddle bag and rubbed the calf down to dry it off.

The cow was lowing, trying weakly to get up. Pecos untied the ropes and she struggled to get on her feet. She couldn't do it. We dragged the now bawling calf and put him in front of the heifer. She got her front legs under her and began to lick the calf from head to toe. We backed off to watch. It wasn't long until the young mother was able to get her unsteady back legs under her and push herself to standing. She swayed like a drunken cowboy but stayed on her feet. She used her nose to guide the calf back to her udder where he began to slurp up his first meal.

"That's a good feelin', compadre."

———————

There was a brand new red brick bank in Clyde now, first State Bank of Clyde, where I had established an account. Things were changing quickly all around us. Abilene had grown from nothing to a thriving community with the arrival of the Texas and Pacific Railroad. It had surpassed Buffalo Gap as the largest community in Taylor County and was pushing hard to become the county seat.

In May we assembled the crew. We went from ranch to ranch until all our friends and neighbors had their calves branded and their market cattle separated. Kelly and Jake Webb moved their chuck wagon from ranch to ranch. Keenan and Kirby had a cousin staying with them. He wasn't a ranch hand, but he could ride a horse and generally stayed out of the way. His name was Remington, like the pistol. He was about fourteen, roughly Keenan's age, and skinny as a rail, with brown hair and big smiling eyes. He was the kind of kid that it was impossible not to like.

We were finishing up on Captain Tyus' place before moving on to mine. The calves had been branded and the bull calves castrated. We didn't have to road brand the cattle, as we planned to drive them only the great distance of six miles to the new loading pens at Clyde. Mr. McClure from Dodge City had telegraphed to make a fair offer for the cattle. We had discussed it and telegraphed our acceptance. The price had reflected the fact that he would have to pay freight to Chicago, but we wouldn't have the expense or time to drive them up the cursed Western Trail. The price of twenty-six dollars seemed about right. There was one last thing to do at the Captain's place. The barren cows needed to be moved in with the market ready steers. The Captain also intended to sell the last of his longhorn bulls.

Remington sat on a pretty little strawberry roan gelding enjoying the beautiful day and watching the cowboys work. There was a rank old bull that charged at the horses, and so far had not been caught by any of the hands due to the six foot spread of his up curving horns. The old brindle bull was pawing dirt over his back, throwing his head and slinging snot. He was really worked up. I made another try at roping him, only to see him throw his head and tail up in the air and run south. Unfortunately, this was right where Remington sat on his horse, completely unaware of the approaching danger.

"Remington, the bull!" I yelled as loud as I could. He looked up, but it was too late.

The bull charged straight into the little roan horse and ran a massive horn through the horse's guts and out the other side. The other horn had Remington penned to the saddle. The boy screamed in pain. The horse squealed his last desperate breath and collapsed. The bull was unable to pull his right horn out and continued to batter Remington and the dying horse.

A pistol shot rang out and Kirby came charging in on his horse firing his pistol as he rode. He placed five .44-40 slugs in the old bull's right chest. The bull bellowed once, fell to his knees and died.

Remington remained trapped. Pecos galloped up with the chuck wagon axe and chopped off the bull's left horn at the base, freeing Remington. His lower leg was twisted in an abnormal shape. It was obvious he had broken both bones. Before we tried to move him, I tied a splint made of two pieces of wood and a couple of pigging strings to hold his leg steady. Pecos and Matt gently eased him out from under the gruesome carnage. Tears rolled from his big eyes, but he didn't cry out. Keenan and Kirby were right beside him.

Kelly rolled up with the chuck wagon and we set the injured boy inside. Kelly drove the wagon, as Keenan, Kirby and I followed on horseback to their mother's house in Belle Plain.

"Kirby, I never seen you shoot so good."

"I guess I never had to before today."

When we arrived at Mrs. Nixon's, we carried him and laid him on a bed. We cut his pants away and saw the crazy way his left leg was twisted. I didn't see any bone sticking out through the skin.

"Kelly, get my old doctor's bag out of the wagon. Boys, I want you to measure from his knee to the ankle, then cut two pieces of smooth wood that long. Wrap them with cloth all the way from end to end. Robin, I need you to tear up about a dozen strips of strong cloth about eighteen inches long."

Kelly returned with the bag. "Pull out that bottle of laudanum."

"I'm gonna guess he weighs between a hundred and a hundred and twenty pounds. Does that sound about right Rem?" He shook his head in agreement. I measured out my best guess of how much laudanum he would need and gave it to him. I waited while it took effect.

Once he was insensible, we pulled his boots off. "Robin, you grab hold right here just below his knee. Hold tight now."

I grabbed his skinny broken leg and pulled straight out. The bones came back together with an audible snap. The pain caused him to open his eyes and groan, but he fell back into his drug-induced sleep. I placed the splints on both sides. I had to have Robin continue to hold his leg so it wouldn't get out of place, while Kelly eased his hand where mine had been to support his ankle. The boys held the splints carefully in place as I wrapped and tied the strips of cloth. The leg held straight after it was splinted. "You two knuckle heads find or make a pair of crutches. Robin, give him two tablespoons of this laudanum whenever he needs it, but not closer than about four hours. Kelly and I got to get back. I'll check on him when I ride through tonight. Boys, stay here with your cousin. We'll finish up without you. Send a telegram for his parents to come on the train to Clyde. He's gonna be in bed a good six weeks."

When we got back to the Captain's place, Kyle had skinned the bull. "I'm gonna get this tanned and give it to Remington."

Another couple of hours of sorting and moving and the cattle at Belle Plain were ready for the road. As my place had the most cattle, we had saved it for last.

I stopped by and checked on Remington. He was propped up eating some soup. I smiled down at the skinny boy who had come so close to being killed by the bull. "How you feelin', Slim?"

"Hi, Mr. Turner, I feel better. That medicine tastes terrible, but it makes it quit hurtin' so bad. My folks will be here in a couple of days to take me home. Thanks for fixin' me up."

We all moved over to my place the next day. It didn't take long to get my spring crop of calves worked with that many people helping. We ran two branding fires. Pecos was roping and dragging calves to one fire and Matt to the other. Courtesy required that they take breaks to allow the others to rope for a while, as this was the position of most fun and honor, at least as long as you didn't miss too often. It was also customary that the owner didn't rope his own stock under normal circumstances. We had some strange ways and customs, but they worked for us. We had the grown cattle already sorted for market.

We stayed near the dugout that night with Kelly and Jake Webb doing the cooking. It was beans, cornbread, and steaks I had supplied. Little Jake did most of the cooking under his father's supervision. Some of the bunch rolled out their bedrolls in the dugout, but I preferred to sleep outside. It was a beautiful night. I smoked my pipe leaning up against the chuck wagon and talked until late with my old friends.

I wouldn't miss the Western Trail this year, especially Comanche Springs. I sure wouldn't miss Dodge City. It would be a simple one day drive into Clyde with the cattle. If we didn't waste too much time, we would all sleep in our own beds that night.

I grabbed an early cup of coffee and some jerky and headed out ahead of the herd to check on Ella and baby Aaron. They were still asleep when I slipped in the back door. I gave the baby and Ella a kiss on the forehead. She woke up and smiled at me. "You be careful. Do you think you'll be home tonight?"

"If everything goes well, I should be, but with cattle you never know. Don't wait up on me."

We had my cattle started out before dawn, when it was just barely light enough to see. We had Pecos and Matt in their customary places up front on the right and left to keep the cattle headed toward the gate. The steers balked a little when they got there, but Pecos and Matt gave them time to sniff the strange opening. They were more than happy to go through, with all the others following. We made it to Captain Tyus' place in an hour and forty-five minutes. We started my cattle just barely up the road past his gate, opening it for the Belle Plain cattle inside the fence. They saw our cattle walking away and were quick to head through the gate and up the road.

The road was fenced on both sides all the way to just outside Clyde. The only place we had to play cowboy was to maneuver them into the shipping pens without wrecking the tidy little town. The railroad agent signed off on my head count. We telegraphed Mr. McClure who responded with a telegram to me and the bank. Within an hour, the bank confirmed the draft and transfer were completed. Those who needed it, drew out money at the bank. There was a nicer type of bar where we shared a drink.

Some stayed behind to see the barber for a haircut and shave, but I headed on home with Pecos, Kyle, Kirby and Keenan. We were back to Belle Plain by half past four. Kyle was ready to see his wife. Keenan and Kirby were worried about Remington. Pecos rode with the boys and me to the Nixon place. Remington was sitting up in bed reading a book. He looked rough, but at least he was improving. The leg looked good, and it was no more swollen than I expected.

Pecos and I lit out over Lytle Gap for home. "Do you miss trailin' cattle to Kansas?"

"Heck, no. I don't miss outlaws, Injuns, crooked gamblers, flooded rivers, quicksand, or storms. Do you miss it?"

"No. This is better. I always felt like we had done somethin' hard, somethin' not everybody could do when we got there with a herd. But this is better."

He stayed for supper, but then went on back to the dugout. I sat out on the porch holding Aaron, talking to Ella, and trying to keep that boy from grabbing my pipe.

Pecos was one of the best men I had ever known with horses. He understood what made them tick. He could work with horses other men had given up on and make something out of them. He had been working with a four year old buckskin that not only bucked, but had taken to rearing up to dislodge a rider. It was a warm clear Friday afternoon. Kirby and Keenan hadn't had to run the freight route that day, so had helped at the ranch. They were watching Pecos work the gelding along with me.

The young horse was not particularly powerfully built, but he was quite agile. His bucking technique was something to see. He was pulling stunts I had never seen. He had dumped Pecos off a couple of times, but Pecos was more than holding his own.

The horse shifted tactics. Since the man on his back wasn't going away from bucking, he'd try rearing up. He would rear up and paw the air. Pecos would spur him to make him run. Around and around the huge round pen they went. The horse threw on the brakes and tried to dislodge his rider over his head. It almost worked, as Pecos was thrown far up onto the horse's neck. Yet the buckskin had failed to dump the rider.

Before Pecos had a chance to get fully reseated, the horse reared high in the air. There was a muddy place on the hard packed ground in the corral where the overhead cypress water tank leaked a tiny spray of water. The horse's feet slipped and he started to fall over backwards. Pecos tried desperately to kick his feet free and get off the saddle, but it happened so fast he didn't have time. The horse fell on top of him. The saddle horn hit him square in the chest. The horse struggled to his feet, but Pecos didn't move.

We ran to him. "Don't move me, Aaron. I'm all busted up inside. I got some papers in the dugout. I'm leaving everything I got to you. We been friends since '62. It's been one hell of a ride." Blood welled up from deep inside him. He gave one violent cough, spewing blood everywhere. That was it. He was gone.

"Ah, Pecos. What have ya done?"

The boys and I carried his limp body to the dugout and laid him out on his bed. I picked up his Winchester from near the door and walked to the corral. I shot that killer horse dead between the eyes. The boys helped me pull the saddle and gear off. I was riding Moon that day. I slipped a rope around the dead horse's neck and dragged him far from the dugout where the coyotes and crows could clean him up.

When I returned, I sent Keenan to get the spring wagon hitched. I undressed the broken body and washed him off real well and redressed him in clean clothes. Kirby helped me wrap him in a quilt my mother had made for him. We laid him in the back of the spring wagon and tied Moon on behind.

The boys rode with me. We stopped and told Ella what had happened. I gave her the little comfort I had to offer, for I knew none myself. We rode on into Belle Plain and laid his body in the little bedroom at the back of the community church building where the travelling preachers sometimes stayed. We sent a telegram to the Methodist preacher who had a new church in Clyde. He soon sent a reply that he would be at the Belle Plain church at ten in the morning. Word spread like wildfire through Belle Plain. Everyone knew and liked Pecos. Those of us who had ridden with him gathered out at Captain Tyus' place and talked until late.

I heard Moon nicker about the time it was getting light. I looked out the bedroom window. All of the trail crew was there near the creek with picks and shovels. They dug a grave in the shade of the pecan grove, being careful not to disturb the flat stone that was simply marked "Baby". They didn't wait to eat, but hurried back into Belle Plain to clean up for the funeral.

Ella and I came in the spring wagon with baby Aaron. The church was packed. Someone had saved us seats on a pew up front. Matt played his guitar. Jake and Kirby joined him on their fiddles. They knew what to play without anyone telling them. They played "Shall We Gather at the River" while the whole congregation sang. I was too upset to do anything but cry in silence.

The minister did a pretty good job. He had asked Mr. Carter, Luke and Levi's father, to lead a prayer. The Captain spoke a few words about what a brave soldier Pecos had been and how he had handled himself in tough situations. They asked me to say a few words, too.

I stood behind the small wooden podium and held on tight to the top. "Pecos Wade went to war with me when I was twelve and he was fifteen. He lost all the family he had in the war and has been part of our family ever since. I never knew him to cheat, steal, or take the Lord's name in vain. He was a fine, brave man. He was your friend. He was my friend. We're gonna miss him."

————

When I came back from the war, my family was pretty well broke. We made our living raising a few cattle, but made our living catching mavericks in the cane breaks and river bottoms. We drove this wild assortment of mostly longhorns up the Shawnee Trail to Sedalia, Missouri in '66. We gathered a herd and took one almost every year after that up the Chisholm Tail to Abilene, Kansas. Now, for the last few years we had driven cattle we had raised on open range to Dodge City, Kansas, up the even more dangerous Western Trail.

The open range had now mostly been fenced. Windmills dotted the prairies. The arrival of the railroad had ended the trail drives. I had seen the dawning day of the cattle kingdom in Texas, and I had seen the sun set on those turbulent days. Trading Texas cattle for Yankee silver dollars had saved Texas from financial collapse. The frontier had rolled forward a hundred miles, right to the foot of the uninhabitable High Plains. Even now there were early steps being taken to subdue the massive dry grassland.

Changes such as barbed wire, windmills, and railroads brought an end to the open range and the days of the cattle kingdom. But ranching would continue to form a vital part of the state's economy and way of life. Like Pecos had said: "It had been one hell of a ride."

————

Not long after Pecos' funeral, I sat smoking my pipe on the front porch, watching the warm twilight fade into darkness. Ella sat next to me, rocking the baby and singing softly to him.

My father had come to Texas in 1817. He had fallen under the spell the wild untamed land. He brought my mother and settled on the Navasota River a few years later. He had fought Indians regularly, outlaws occasionally, and had fought in the Texas Revolution and the Mexican-American War. He had died when I was one year and one day old. I had come to know him through the memories of others. He had left a legacy of courage, integrity, generosity and kindness.

All the things he had fought so hard to gain were threatened in the War Between the States. I had ridden away with my brothers and friends to save Texas and the South from the grasping hands of the blue coated Yankees. I left a brother and many friends where they had fallen far from home.

I had returned to find our very life and liberty still threatened by the victorious North. We had struggled to find the necessities of daily living. We found ourselves unable to hold office, vote or serve on a jury. It was a bad time for Texas. It was a bad time for the Turners.

We gathered wild cattle and drove them north to sell for the hard earned dollars we needed to pay taxes and buy groceries. We struggled, but we survived. We fought Comanche, Kiowa and Cheyenne, but God had seen fit to spare us. We had battled with outlaws of every kind, but the worst had been the Ku Klux Klan.

We had moved to the farthest edge of the Texas frontier and established our ranch and our home. We had endured drought, blizzards, stampedes and storms. We had seen friends and family slip away before our eyes. But we had persevered, never giving up. My family had set roots deep in the soil of Texas. That soil had been enriched with our sweat, our tears and our blood. But those roots held fast through all the storms that life had thrown at us. We had persisted and carved out a way of life.

I looked at Ella as she nursed the baby. His bare feet stuck out from under the blanket. He spread and wiggled in toes as he ate. Here was our future, this child, and children and generations yet unborn. I was living to leave a legacy, not of land and cattle, but of values and character, that would carry on through the future. The circle would not be broken.